I0618025

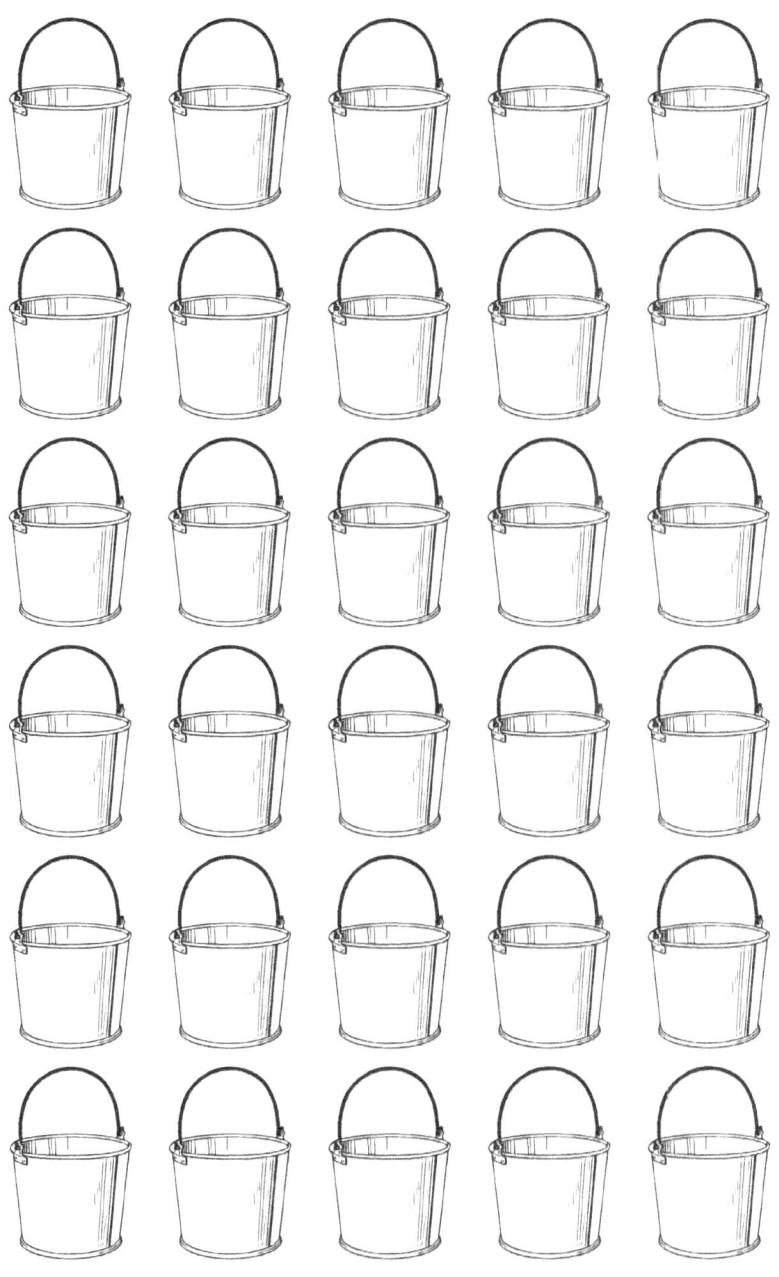

Pure Slush Books

2014
March

Vol. 3

a Pure Slush book

Pure
Slush

March 2014 Vol. 3 is edited by Matt Potter and
published by Pure Slush, January 2014.

All stories are copyright © of the individual authors

Cover photograph copyright © Jasmaine Mathews
http://www.flickr.com/photos/poofy/

ISBN: 978-1-925101-17-1

All rights reserved.

You can find *Pure Slush* at http://pureslush.webs.com

Copies of all *Pure Slush* publications can be bought
at http://pureslush.webs.com/store.htm

All queries re *Pure Slush* can be made
via email to edpureslush@live.com.au

A note on differences in punctuation and spelling

Pure Slush proudly features (both online and in print) writers from all over the English–speaking world. Some speak and write English as their first language, while for others, it's their second or third or even fourth language. Naturally, across all versions of English, there are differences in punctuation and spelling, and even in meaning. These differences are reflected in the stories *Pure Slush* publishes, and it accounts for any differences in punctuation, spelling and meaning found within these pages.

stories by

Guilie Castillo–Oriard

Townsend Walker

Derek Osborne

Gloria Garfunkel

John Wentworth Chapin

Lynn Beighley

Andrew Stancek

Rachel Ambrose

Gill Hoffs

Susan Tepper

Jessica McHugh

Shane Simmons

Michelle Elvy

Len Kuntz

Michael Webb

James Claffey

Gwendolyn Joyce Mintz

Stephen V. Ramey

Gay Degani

Sally–Anne Macomber

Mandy Nicol

Margaret Bingel

Darryl Price

Teresa Burns Gunther

Matt Potter

Gary Percesepe

Nathaniel Tower

Kimberlee Smith

Vanessa Weibler Paris

Joanne Jagoda

h. l. nelson

for

Nancy Chapple,

for her keen eye

and diligence

M.P.

Dive   Guilie Castillo–Oriard   15

La Ronde / Joey and Annie   Townsend Walker   21

The Moment   Derek Osborne   25

The Crash   Gloria Garfunkel   30

Azure   John Wentworth Chapin   32

Punch Drunk   Lynn Beighley   37

After the Flood   Andrew Stancek   41

That Awkward Moment   Rachel Ambrose   44

Rory's Glory   Gill Hoffs   46

Swoon   Susan Tepper   51

Shady Grace   Jessica McHugh   53

Rotted Leaves, Wilted Flowers   Shane Simmons   57

Canary   Michelle Elvy   61

Trail's End   Len Kuntz   66

Third Inning   Michael Webb   70

Petals and Perfume   James Claffey   73

The Lucky Ones   Gwendolyn Joyce Mintz   78

The Comedian   Stephen V. Ramey   81

Father and Son   Gay Degani   87

Schöne Grüße aus Tirol   Sally–Anne Macomber   92

Candles   Mandy Nicol   94

Dreaming   Margaret Bingel   95

Big Words   Darryl Price   97

Another Man   Teresa Burns Gunther   99

The Mystery of the Opium Den   Matt Potter   104

Shot   Gary Percesepe   109

Samford gets a rectal exam   Nathaniel Tower   115

Reunion   Kimberlee Smith   120

Winter Weight   Vanessa Weibler Paris   128

The Blind Date   Joanne Jagoda   131

Rinse and Repeat   h. l. nelson   136

Authors   143

Saturday, 1st March 2014

Dive

by Guilie Castillo–Oriard

Under the palapa roof of the school's terrace, the dive instructor with ridiculously sun–bleached curls brings the briefing to its merciful end. Luis Villalobos swallows a caustic cheer. He'd be in a better mood if he'd stopped at Barista for a cappuccino, but there was barely time to shower before Wendolyn showed up.

He sneaks a look at her. Like the other two diver wannabes at the picnic table, she's hanging on each of the instructor's words, simpering like a groupie.

The instructor – Jan from Amsterdam, which rhymes pronounced the Dutch way, the stress on the *dam*, the short *a* – rubs his hands in a bad imitation of a wicked witch. "Let's check if you've been paying attention. What's the first rule of diving?"

"Keep blowing bubbles!"

Luis's knee jiggles under the table impatiently. He – Wendolyn, too – should be at the office. Milena seems pleased with the results of the FATCA project so far, but she expected nothing. She had to be wrestled in, and now she's broadcasting each success to the Ehrlich mothership in Singapore as if it was all her initiative. She won't be so eager to claim credit a month from now, when Ehrlich's credibility is in shreds before the US Treasury.

No. A month from now it'll all be on Luis.

But it's Carnaval. The halls of Ehrlich Fiduciary stand deserted. His FATCA task force is otherwise engaged: teener parade, children's parade, main parade, costumes, rehearsals. He laughed at first, until Marco from HR sat him down and explained about this most sacrosanct of Curaçao celebrations. And so, exasperated, he let Wendolyn rope him into being her buddy today. *Buddy*. Next he'll be best *pals* with Jan from Amsterdam.

"All right!" Mr. Amster*dam* claps once and gets up, nods at the six−foot−eight dive master on the terrace steps. "Guillaume will get you your gear."

"You excited?" Wendolyn brushes his arm as they fall behind the giant Guillaume. Her judicious flirting is still subtle enough to be ignorable. Luis hopes, somewhat ruefully, it stays that way.

The other two novices, an American couple on their honeymoon − Who takes a diving course on a *honeymoon*? − save Luis from lying. "We're excited," the girl says, and tugs on her child−husband's arm. "Aren't we, Robbie?"

"Stoked, man." Robbie grins at Luis. "You?"

Luis rolls out a smile, more charity than irony. "Totally stoked."

"Hey Luis?" Jan pronounces it Louise. An improvement; usually he gets Loo−is. "Hold up a sec. You look a little out of it. You okay?"

An honorable exit. But Wendolyn's still within earshot, so he says, "Yeah. No, I'm fine. Just − late night."

Jan looks him over, nods. "Drank a lot?"

"Ten, twelve beers." He had eight.

Jan flips through the medical histories on his clipboard. "You smoke, huh? But no cardio history, no back problems, no regular headaches. Except for now?"

Luis obliges with a chuckle.

"You in good shape? Physically?"

Luis shrugs, nods.

"Fifty push−ups, soldier."

"Seriously?" Hope rises. He'll never make it past five.

Jan chucks him on the shoulder. "Nah. But I want you close to me, understand? Your eyes, on me, all the time."

"Actually −" Luis lowers his voice even though Wendolyn has disappeared into the equipment room. "I'm not feeling so hot. Maybe it's best if I −"

"No chickening out, man. It's just an intro dive. You'll be fine."

Guillaume is waiting, holds up a pair of boots. "You are 11, yes? Try these booties."

Booties?

The rest of the equipment comes with grown−up names. Wetsuit − XL, because the L felt like medieval testicular torture. Buoyancy control device − BC in divespeak − that hinders everything, protects nothing. The dive master tugs at three of the hundred straps on the vest−like thing and decrees, "It fits." Flippers − more straps. Mask − another strap.

So that's that. Luis is expected to survive underwater in boots, a wetsuit that − regardless of what size the tag says − still feels too tight, and an inflatable lifesaver that requires more assistance than Marie Antoinette's corsets. As a plot twist, Guillaume tucks four two−kilo metal blocks into the thing's pockets.

"Guillaume will assemble your gear today." Jan stands over the giant kneeling on the sand in front of six tanks, each a tad smaller than the dive master's thighs. "Intro courtesy only. If you sign up for the course, you'll learn how to do it yourselves next time."

No next time for Luis, and for that he feels immense gratitude.

Short−lived. "Luis." Jan is crooking a finger at him. "Over here."

Guillaume holds up a tank with Luis's BC strapped to it. Jan parts the snarl of nylon and velcro to reveal an armhole of sorts.

He adjusts and clasps and clicks Luis into place. "How does that feel?"

Luis wriggles his shoulders. "Like a straitjacket."

Jan snorts. "Pussy. Guillaume?"

The giant lets go of the tank. The vest tightens against Luis's shoulders and stomach. "Ooof. No, it's good." He hates that he sounds so strained.

The walk down the beach to the surf, all twenty steps, is a purgatory of awkwardness. The wetsuit is hot. The tank bumps the back of his legs. His feet feel clumsy in the boots. The harness velcroed at his waist makes a ripping noise with every breath. The rubber hoses spouting from the regulator, aptly nicknamed octopus, tangle his arms. One hooks up to the BC. Another ends in a gauge with numbers in the thousands that mean nothing to Luis. Two other hoses, one yellow, one black, end in mouthpieces. Jan folds the yellow into one of the myriad BC pockets. Luis fishes behind him for the black one, studies the mouthpiece, turns away from the happy crowd. He hopes it's been cleaned properly. It tastes rubbery. He breathes in, gets nothing.

"Tank is not yet open." Guillaume pats his shoulder, fumbles behind Luis's head. "Oh−kay. Try now again?"

Luis takes a tentative pull, gets a loud life−support sucking sound. And air! Funny−tasting. Dry. Drier than normal, at least. He will never again take that lovely, effortless provision of oxygen for granted.

He's not cut out for this. The only reason he doesn't call it quits is because he's certain he'll never be able to get out of this torture chamber people call diving gear on his own. He's equally certain Jan and Guillaume will be happy to set him free − once they've shown the Three Enthusiasts the marvels of life underwater.

Ocean, finally. The water feels so good on his skin, sautéed in sweat beneath the wetsuit. He dunks his head, soaks off the grumpiness. Taste of salt on his lips. Sound of baby waves kissing the beach. Photoshopped blue of this ocean.

"Inflate your BCs," Jan says somewhere to the left. "Luis! Where you going, man?"

Luis has drifted on the current. He floats back to where the others are standing in waist−deep water, on his back to keep the tank's nozzle from poking a hole at the base of his skull.

Jan takes hold of his vest and drags him into position between Guillaume and him. "Remember our deal? With me. All the time." He gropes at the hose on Luis's shoulder. Again the life−support whoosh but somewhat muted. "How does that feel?"

Like the hand of King Kong crushing his ribs. Panic subsides when Luis realizes he now floats without effort. "Good. Yeah."

Jan readjusts straps, checks the gauge, fiddles with the tank, hands Luis the black mouthpiece. "Check your air. Can you breathe?"

Whooooosh. Luis sounds like Darth Vader. Probably looks like him, too. Hard to talk with that thing in your mouth. Luis gives Jan a thumbs−up.

Jan rolls his eyes. "That means up. Get your signals straight."

Right. They covered hand signals in the briefing. Luis makes a circle of thumb and forefinger, the universal OK sign.

"Good boy. All right, everyone over here, please. We're going to do some drills underwater, get you comfortable, then we'll head out to the reef. Okay?"

The Enthusiast Chorus holds up comically identical finger circles. "Okay!"

Forty minutes later, six heads bob back up onto the surface. Six faint splashes. The whoosh of six BCs inflating. The pop of six regulator mouthpieces being spit out. Six faces marked raccoon−

style from the masks. And the eyes, the telltale eyes: four pairs brimming with the high of boundaries breached.

Luis wriggles his jaw, winces. He must've been clenching that mouthpiece too hard.

Jan is looking at him. Is that a glint of pride in his eye?

Head still full of the great blue below, the thrill of weightlessness (even though Jan had to add four more kilos to convince this lily–livered, oxygen–addicted body to sink), a feeling of having returned, the prodigal child, to a primeval state of grace, Luis grins. Already in love with the pain in his jaw.

"When can we do this again?"

Sunday, 2ⁿᵈ March 2014

La Ronde / Joey and Annie

by Townsend Walker

Joey drives into the parking lot of Comfort Suites, there, off Route 21, looking for Annie's green Mini. A tradition, short−lived (two months), for Annie to go to the motel, check in, park her car in front of their room, change into something comfortable (she's been raiding Victoria's Secret), wait for him.

He opens the door. He sees Annie, a cat stretched across the bed, blonde hair fanned out on the maroon spread, giving him a what−are−you−standing−there−for look with her eyebrows, uncurling her legs, sitting up to lure him with the full effect of her latest bit of flimsy red lace. He doesn't see the Everyman motel room, its green shag rug, molded wood particle furniture (always in white−beige, sometimes mottled), wide screen TV, or popcorn ceiling.

The magnet force of the lingerie and what is barely hidden pull Joey across the room.

"Can I unwrap my present now."

"Only if you untie the bows carefully."

An hour later.

"That was nice," she says.

"We should do it more often." As soon as the platitude slips out, he knows better.

"That's what I keep telling you. Two afternoons a week is not enough. How serious are you about us?"

"Serious enough to drive fifty miles in the snow telling Sonia and the kids that I had to take some papers to my accountant."

Facing Sonia's wrath for leaving the family on a Sunday afternoon. *What? Your accountant doesn't work during the week? And in this snow? Get a new one.*

"I brought those receipts you asked for."

Joey stretches his arm out from under the covers to open his briefcase and fumbles for the files he brought.

"Not here, you idiot."

The files move from his hand to her hand to her nightstand and will be forgotten when they leave the room.

Annie is, in fact, the accountant for Joey's moving business; has been for some months, since she moved from Los Angeles, transferred by PricewaterhouseCoopers to the Newark office. Joey's friend Max recommended her. *A great accountant, a great rack. Enjoy.*

Yes, a great accountant: nailed everything he'd hidden in the books (Sonia's car, kids' schools, trip to Bermuda) first time through the accounts. Then told him how he was going to come clean with it costing him a dime more in taxes.

On the second count of the recommendation: they'd both been invited to a New Year's Eve party, sparks ignited during a casual dance, dampened by Sonia's presence of course, but two days later Annie called, suggested lunch at the Hilton. Dessert followed in Room 634.

Joey thinks he needs to stop this fling with Annie; thinks about it when he drives home after being with her; the kids crash into him with hugs when he opens the door; when he's with Mamma and Papa (married fifty years); with Sonia making love (Annie's eagerness to get to bed, Sonia's reluctance; Annie moves, Sonia responds): he isn't going to screw up the kids with a messy divorce, which he knows it would be.

He props himself up on his elbow. Even with smeared lipstick, Annie's mouth beckons. It's change—the—subject time, Joey tells himself.

"Hey, somebody asked me about Max the other day. You see him recently, know how I can get in touch? We were close, but last couple of months I haven't seen him around."

Joey tells Annie about this friend of his sister Gina (leaves out the part about his college affair with Madge) who is looking to get her husband offed because he is beating the shit out of her. Looking for a hit man and this Madge doesn't run in those circles. Paying good, mid five figures, could go higher.

"Why doesn't she go to the cops?"

"This guy is rich as Croesus, but she'd end up with squat—all and miserable for years having to deal with him and custody arrangements."

"So you're asking your accountant, partner track at a Big Four firm, to find a hit man? Not really my line of work."

"All I need is to get in touch with Max."

She stretches her legs, rolls on top of him and sits up.

"I do other things in my spare time. Show me *your* hit man routine."

An hour later.

"Jeezus, look at the time. Sonia is going to have a cow."

"Not for me to delay you, lover boy, but what do you want me to tell Max if I run across him?"

Joey gives her the info he got from his sister Gina. Guy's name is Franklin Lancaster Cabot III; goes by Frank. Works at Goldman Sachs on West Street, downtown. Six foot three, 200 pounds, pasty complexion, curly black hair going gray, beak for a nose, Brooks Brothers dresser, loafers with tassels. And Hermes ties, the silly patterned ones. Outside, Prada Aviators, high–end sunglasses, blue tint, even in a March snow storm.

"We need to talk before you go."

Joey has his pants up to his knees.

"What about?"

She kneels on the bed and wraps the red lace around her.

"What I asked you before. Where do you see us going?"

Joey's trying for a little obliviousness by focusing on zipping up his pants.

"I don't know, honey. I enjoy being with you. I know that. No one's ever been as good as you." *Maybe Madge,* hoping the thought doesn't show.

Annie puts her hands on his shoulders and leans her forehead into his.

"Listen carefully, you are going to think about us and on Thursday you will give me your decision: me or her." Unsaid, his business is on the line too.

Joey calls Gina on the way back from the motel, tells her he's made a contact for Madge. Gina asks who; Joey won't say, Gina asks how Frank was described; Joey goes though the litany, suddenly throws the phone on the other side of the car as a screech comes through the speaker, "Not pasty, not pasty, tanned, tanned, go back and tell them tanned!"

Joey figures: *whatever.*

Monday, 3rd March 2014

The Moment

by Derek Osborne

They made it as far as Annapolis before Max went in for the first round of chemo. Pancreatic carcinoma, locally advanced, too late to operate, a drawback from being in such good shape, the body masks the problem in borrowing strength from other organs, other systems, by the time you think something's wrong the cancer has moved in for good.

He's been there a week, Sloan–Kettering in Manhattan. His room faces the East River and he's got a great view of Hell Gate, that narrow part of the channel behind the UN where tugs and barges pass one another while battling six knots of current. There's always something to watch, always some mayhem but mostly he sleeps, pukes and sleeps. Pam, his sister, comes every day; Andi, his youngest daughter, a student at NYU, comes with her iPad and shows him the film she's been editing for class.

He and Rebecca talk every night. She left that morning down in Miami but called before boarding the plane. She's out in LA doing a season's worth of *Miami Blue* interiors. She'll be getting a break the end of the month and coming back out. Max hasn't told her yet; Eddie's been sworn upon pain of death. Max and Rebecca are having a blast, telling each other their childhood stories, how she got started in television, what it was like to move from Chile to Miami at age nine. Max talks mostly about the boat, his glory days in school, he's never talked to anyone about the war, and for obvious reasons, he avoids his wife's battle with her own cancer. He's told Rebecca the basics but that's about it. He'd much rather listen. They're like a couple of teenagers, even playing the game of who'll hang up first, who gets the last goodbye. She has no idea how her voice affects him, but he can't go down that road. They've both made a promise not to go near what Max began on the boat. If one of them even gets close the other changes the subject. When they hang up Max lulls himself to sleep in the echoes of her words, watching the boats on the river, the red and green navigational lights moving below in the dark. At night, on the ward, things grow quiet. Every so often the rattle of carts and shuffle of rubber-soled shoes come racing down the hall. Sometimes, in the morning, the room where they went is empty, no flowers or knick-knacks along the window, the white board erased, the bed too neat.

Max does not dwell, for him it's another Monday and he's getting out tomorrow. He'll be able to continue the therapy at home. He hasn't told them home is a ninety foot ketch tied up in Annapolis, that home will be sailing next week to Nantucket. Max is still in the initial stages. Like everyone else he's Googled the graph and seen the survival rates. He's doing what all good sailors do in a storm – he's clearing the decks, battening down, watching the sky and the radar – he knows the boat, knows the odds, knows that God is coming but God has come before and he's always survived. Why should this be different?

The SAT phone rings. It's not his sister; she's been using the room phone ever since he yelled about spending two dollars a minute just because it's convenient. He gets up from his chair by the window, rolls the little blue robot back to the night stand and checks the phone's screen. It's coming from somewhere in Kansas. It's also coming from an altitude of forty-two thousand feet. He's so used to that number reading zero, sea-level, he notices immediately.

"Hello?" he says, pressing the big red button.

"Hi, it's me."

Max lets the voice sink in. "You're in Kansas?"

"How did you know? Maybe. I'm on the CBS jet."

"Really?" he says.

"We'll be in DC around seven."

"Really?"

"I don't need to be back on set till Thursday so I hitched a ride."

"You celebrities," Max says, teasing, "Just hop on the jet whenever you like."

She's laughing. He closes his eyes, sitting there on the edge of the bed. One of the nurses has come in to check. He's pretty sure the robot tells them whenever he moves; like *Gadabout's* GPS, it sounds an alarm whenever the anchor is dragging.

"You're still in Annapolis, right?" Rebecca says.

"You got on a plane without checking?"

"I had Anja call Eddie."

"And what did Eddie say?"

"He said you were somewhere in town."

"I'm in New York."

"Oh no?"

"Up here on business."

"Oh no?"

Max is doing some quick calculations. He's already had the coaching concerning his discharge. All he needs is the meds and paraphernalia. He can call Doctor Bloom and get them now.

"It's okay," he says, "I'll drive down tonight after dinner."

That should allow enough time. It's only a four−hour drive but he might need to stop and rest − or puke.

"You're sure it's okay?"

He's imagining her there on the boat, curled up on the sofa in the salon. It was designed to be more of a library, complete with a tiled hearth and freestanding furniture. The dining table, usually center in most big yachts, is offset to starboard and gives the illusion of two separate rooms, each with a six foot skylight

27

above, Herreshoff interior, raised panels painted off-white, all of it trimmed in cherry.

"Max?" she says when he doesn't answer, "I just did it. I heard the suits were going and barely had time to pack."

"It couldn't be more perfect."

"Oh Max."

It just comes, for both of them, they never know when.

"No tears, Becca, we can finally be together."

All this time, months, and they haven't even kissed. The nurse sees his face and whispers she'll be back. Max is thinking on his feet now, trying to work things out.

"Eddie's going to pick you up. If you're wheels down at seven you'll get back to the boat around nine. You should miss most of rush hour. If I make my excuses and leave dinner early I'll be able to get there by midnight, unless I hit traffic on the Jersey Turnpike, they're doing construction all up and down ... Becca, you listening?"

"Who are you having dinner with?"

Max can be fast on his feet.

"One of your competitors."

"Bastard," she says, "Which one?"

"I shouldn't say."

"I'll get it out of you."

The flirting is so much fun. Everything else disappears.

"Now say goodbye and hang up," she says.

"You first."

"One of the guys wants to use the phone. They're having a conference call."

"They can do that?"

"It's a G5."

"Of course it's a G5."

"See you soon."

Out on the river a bright yellow tug is pushing a line of blue barges. The barges are filled with stone, deep in the water, pushing a huge white wave. Coming the other direction is a forty−foot sloop, a small yacht taking advantage of the tide, probably traveling ten knots and everyone hanging on for dear life as the boat pitches and yaws in the steep chop. The tug is at full throttle, black smoke shooting from its angled twin stacks, kicking a good−sized wake that only grows larger when fighting the current. A ten−foot face has formed, a regular surf as the sailboat bellies down in the trough. They climb the face, see−saw the crest, crash down the backside flipping up into the air, all of them landing again in a jumble of red foul weather gear and confusion of lines. The sails rattle. The guy at the wheel sees they've made it and raises both hands in triumph. The others join in. The tug sounds its horn. Max can just hear it through the glass. *They're having the time of their lives*, he's thinking. He looks down at the dull gray screen of the phone. In little black letters up in the right hand corner it reads, STANDBY.

He looks around the room, the clean white walls, the molded plastic furniture, the white board telling him who he is, who is his nurse, the room and telephone number. It's Monday, March 3rd.

"Come on, Pam," he says, "Where's that call when I need it?"

Tuesday, 4th March 2014

The Crash

by Gloria Garfunkel

Depressed Ralph here. I started crying constantly on Valentine's Day and haven't stopped since. I'm in a Depression Coma, can't get out of bed, have taken a sick leave. Have nothing to say except that I am a big fucking failure who can't even keep New Year's Resolutions.

I am malfunctioning on so many different levels at once. No one at work knows I'm bipolar and I want to keep it that way. I lost a job telling everyone I was bipolar once, believing it was just like revealing I was gay and they couldn't discriminate. People freaked. I've heard of other horror stories like mine of people telling colleagues leading to firing under all sorts of false pretenses, calling normal behaviors "symptoms". Admitting you are bipolar is admitting you are unreliable and impulsive with poor judgment and distorted thinking no matter how excellent you are at your job. No, I would never tell a soul. And believe me, it's not paranoia. The Americans with Disabilities Act is totally hopeless when it comes to standing up for Bipolar Disorder. Only geniuses and actresses get tolerated for being bipolar. It's even cool for them.

Chloe doesn't work where I do. Seeing me in a more subdued state of mind changed Chloe's view of me and she's decided to stick around. She thinks my cycling mood swings are like her father's and it is her job to save my life.

Wait until she witnesses my Mixed Mood Episode, when I have manic energy while feeling horribly depressed, irritable and angry with racing paranoid thoughts. If that doesn't scare her off, nothing will. I can feel it coming on.

Wednesday, 5th March 2014

Azure

by John Wentworth Chapin

Charles wishes he wasn't angry, but he is: angry at India, angry at the yoga center, angry at himself. He is angry at Esther, who talked him into coming here. As he prepares to add to the angry list, the woman in a sari next to him loudly vacuums a bolus of snot from her sinuses, then hocks it into her mouth. She turns her back to Charles and fusses with the bus window, sliding it open enough to spit out the window. She daubs at her mouth with the end of the sari draped over her shoulder.

Charles tugs the signal wire, catapulting himself away from the woman and toward the front of the bus, which stops almost immediately. Charles sees the deep blue ribbon of ocean beckoning beyond the same string of derelict buildings he has seen everywhere, and he steps off the bus. When he was meditating in this oppressive swampy heat just an hour ago, he had to put aside any thoughts of sweat, to ignore the heat and the flies and the smell of the people around him and just *sit*. They told him to cultivate awareness: *thoughts are just thoughts – push them aside.* Thoughts are one thing, but a numbness in your asscheeks and a mosquito in your ear is another.

Instead of feeling a wave of relief, he is immediately aware of all the misfortunes his impulsiveness could invite: lost, robbed, sold into white slavery. He ditched his yoga−meditation−vegan retreat. He ditched his bus. He has a useless iPhone, a useful wallet, a passport, a handful of foreign coins he can't easily count, and a girlishly tiny knapsack holding underwear, soap, a condom, phone charger, and a toothbrush. He's only a couple of miles south of Chennai, an easy walk; he can see the lump of taller buildings at the city center, a long strip of beach connecting him and the city.

He runs toward the beach. The sun pounds on him, but the ocean is *right there*, so he keeps running. When he stops at the pounding blue waves, he doesn't dare leave his things on the beach for the hordes to pilfer. He empties his pockets into the knapsack and wades waist deep into the ocean, holding flip−flops and sack and shirt above his head. Despite the balancing act, the water cools him.

"I don't do well with discomfort," Charles said, frowning at the yoga retreat website they looked at on his iPad.

Esther read the screen in silence. Yoga and meditation sounded too much like religion for her peace of mind. She wanted answers, not hocus−pocus.

"I guess I mean more like with *challenges* or *difficulty*," he said. "If your life is easy and then it is suddenly hard, it's still *hard*, you know?"

The old woman still stared at him, reclined in her mechanical hospital bed set up in her dining room.

"You're judging me," he said.

"I don't see why you need *my* sympathy to get through *your* life," she said, snapping the words.

"I don't know why you think telling you my problems is looking for sympathy," he answered. He was fully aware that she lost the ability to walk and possibly even her mind in a car accident a couple of months earlier, an accident − which she caused and he witnessed − that killed three people. But *still*.

"I have far better things to do than tiptoe around your attitude. Why don't you just go ahead and go to the meditation retreat? What's the worst that could happen?" Esther said, tiredness front and center.

He answered, "I have been reading a lot of women's confessional memoirs lately. I guess the worst is that I won't find what I am looking for."

"You won't know if it was a good or bad decision until you go. If you don't go, you will never know."

Charles realized that she just made the decision for him. "What does the other side of the world have that I can't find in Baltimore?" he asked.

Esther brushed from her forehead a strand of gray hair lighter than her dark skin. "Go find out," she said.

Charles is wrong about the beach. It doesn't go all the way to the city center. A barrier of blue cuts across the sand, the mouth of a lagoon or river. He considers trying to cross it, but his phone could get wet or he could be eaten by crocodiles. He doesn't know if there are crocodiles, but since he can see a bridge not too far inland, it doesn't seem worth it.

He walks a few blocks away from the beach, searching for a road to the bridge. He comes across a temple with garishly bright sculpted columns of gods and fruit and animals. A throng gathers outside: old and young, saris and jeans, t—shirts and suits. Most of them have marks on their foreheads, either carefully drawn dots or smudges of color. He should join them, abandon himself to the masses, but he is too pissy right now for noise and people. It's hot. It stinks. He can't.

He walks until he finds a major thoroughfare and follows it north, pleased with himself when he discovers the exact bridge he saw from the beach. Halfway across the bridge, he stops to survey the beach, the river/lagoon, the city ahead of him. He catches his breath. *I have good instincts.*

That brings him to two hours earlier, when he was sitting in meditation for the second full day, increasingly agitated that he wanted to shut off his mind, but he couldn't. Flies and awful heat and stench assaulted him and he couldn't bear the feeling of his own fingertips touching his own thumbs in meditation, but that was camouflage. In the misery of silence, on the other side of the world, he couldn't escape his only thought: *you are wasting your life and the clock is ticking and you have nothing to show for it.*

But here I am! he shouted at the void. *Doing this!*

The void did not respond but the accusation echoed. *You are wasting your life.*

He spies a flash of bright blue along the water's edge, a strange bird. When he squints, a peacock comes into focus. Are there wild peacocks? He doesn't know the answer, and he can't look it up on his phone. The peacock disappears behind tall, dark brush, returning Charles to himself on the bridge.

He doesn't quite know what to do with himself. The five days before his flight were to be filled with meditation and pathfinding. Now he's suspended between sky and water with two possible paths.

He continues north, sweat−soaked. The walk is good for him, although suddenly it is very crowded on the street. He thinks it's time now to find a cab or a hotel but the crush of bodies around him becomes greater, another throng of people swept up in religious fervor. This is what he wants: ecstasy and spectacle, animal sacrifice and widow−burning and fire−walking. This is why he has come to India, after all. Isn't it?

Charles walks with the crowd, now spilling into the road and stopping traffic. They move like floodwaters around trucks and cars. Time has ended, the world around the crowd frozen as the throng surges on toward its ecstatic finale.

The crowd comes to the foot of a soaring white building. The people behind press up into the mayhem, some funneling through the open doors of the building, some people streaming out, fresh dark marks on their foreheads. *Yes*, thinks Charles, surrendering himself. *I'm ready for it.* He closes his eyes as the crowd carries him forward: feeling, hearing, smelling. Inside the building, he breathes incense and hears familiar music, prompting him to look more carefully around.

He's in a church, a soaring white cathedral, in a line of people streaming up to the altar where they receive a quick daub of gray ash on their foreheads from a priest. There are only two white men in the place: Charles and a blue−robed Saint Thomas statue.

He has come all the way around the world to a goddamned Catholic church. Charles turns and crashes back through the surging crowd, out the door, down the steps, and onto the street. At the edge of the crowd, he pauses to catch his breath. "Fuck!" he exclaims, half out of breath with frustration.

A man about his age, skin darker than the ash on his forehead, catches Charles's eye. "Friend," the man calls, "what are you giving up for Lent?"

"Religion," Charles replies, standing straight. He walks north to the city under the hot, blue sky.

Thursday, 6th March 2014

Punch Drunk

by Lynn Beighley

Best night on tevee, right? Thast what they say whoever they are. Excuse my wine glass has somehowb ecome emptied.

Better. and I just pullled the phone cord out from the wall because pieople won't quit calling and calling because ITS FRiCKING LUV WEEEK/

I mean on that realty show with Bulldozer Plover its all about the love. love week can bite me.

My dad is here. Its he's cool about me drinking, he thinks i'm a riot. I am so so ANGRY and Im also really scared okay? wht is bill going to say in a minute, I don't think I want to watch. But I cant not.

Dad's got pollock on his lap and is petting her and shes all happy and he's all happy and the only one in the entire wolrd who's not happy is me. I've got my chat cliet open on my lap, I mean on my computer on my lap. Not close to as nice as having a cat one wons lap, but okay. ON the othere end of my chat is Seamus.

Seamus: You think America will make him propose to you? I can't imagine anything more romantic!

Me: bite me

Seamus: Maybe you can have the ceremony during the final show of the season! It'll be perfect, America and call in and tell you both how to answer to I DO. Oh oh OH and

Me: fuck u

Seamus: there'll be a cliffhanger, where America chooses if you get to use birth control on your honeymoon to wherever they vote for you to go (I'm thinking Disneyworld, so romantical!), or if you'll have America's FIRST CROWDSOURCED BABY! That's a WHOLE NEW SERIES.

Seamus is a giants dickhole. I strat to pound out a very obsene reply but Dad's leanig over and trying tosee my screen so I close it. and show's on. FUCK

Ther's a teaser part with Bill. He looks okay, they cleaned him up preetty good for this but still, meh.

"Next we hear from Bill with his love question for you this week," greasy announcr guy says. I hate the host guy even though he's farking hot. Afater all this is over i'm going to get bill to interoduce me to him

So Bill. It's been a few weeks since YOU TELL ME strted and so far Bills spiffed up his wardrobe and gotten a lot less annoyiong at work all because of the way America answered the poll questions for him. Iand he's so funny because he says he has to do what America tells him to do because it wouldn't be right otherwise. So whem AMERICA told him to him to go all GQ and the show bouth him the clothes and stuff he did it. Look, I'm not a fan of trends whatever but he looks so much better without the crap he used to wear.

"Was that him? He looks really sharp." my dad asks during the cialis commercial.

"I'm going to update my Match Dot Com profile photograph, do you think he would help me buy an outfit for it? Oh, and I need to refill my Cialis."

swear to god my dad's a freak and I'm ready to scream but instead I get more wine wine because bill because FUCKING LOVE WEEK . at least I trya to but things are spinny so i sit down

and Bill

Bill: Yes, Mark, there is a particular young lady I have had my eye on for some time. She seems as though we would be quite compatible. However, there's the difficulty of her being my coworker to overcome, so I 'haven't made my move' as some people say. As well as, he pauses, her tendency to laugh inappropriately. She has a terrible sense of humor.

WHAT DO YOU MEAN TERRIBLE YOU WEASLEASS I yell and my dad says OW as Pollock sinks her claws in his leg in frigth. And it hits me

coworker fuck fuck fuck fuck fuck fuck I zone out and don't really here waht else he says. he mand mark go back and fortht. I hear GINGER nad I start cussing out loud until my dad puts hims arm around me amd pull sme close. I love my dad even if he's a dating freak and smells like old spice and onions.

And my atteniot returns to hthe teevee when I hear

Smarmy Mark: I'd say it's time we let America decide. AMERICA, HERE ARE YOUR OPTIONS:

A) BILL GETS TO GO OUT WITH A DREAM DATE YOU, AMERICA, CHOOSES FOR HIM !

B) BILL ASKS OUT HIS GINGER−HAIRED COWORKER WITH THE LOUSY SENSE OF HUMOR!

C) BILL'S LOVE LIFE GOES NOWHERE THIS WEEK

we won't know the answer for almost an hour and I'm sleep

It's morning and I'm on my couch in the clothes from last night and oh my god does my head hurt. I'm covered with a blanket and a note from my dad is pinned to it. Before I open it, I feel my cell phone vibrate and I slowly pull it from my pocket.

"I hear there are treatments for impaired humor tolerances," says Seamus. "I'd say Billyboy pegged you right off. You signed off just as I was on a roll, Ginger."

"Not so loud," I say. "I committed suicide by alcohol poisoning last night, be a little bit respectful of the dearly departed." It's already after 9, crap. Must hurry.

"So what are you wearing?"

"Um, excuse me?"

"For your big day. You've got to look pretty for the cameras, Red."

Dear AMERICA, bite me.

After the Flood

by Andrew Stancek

The problem is language. I am extraordinary with feelings, with observation, with picking up nuances of emotion between people. I am even better with birds now. I sense the slightest reverberation, too fine for a human instrument to calibrate, like a sound perfectly audible to dogs but nonexistent for humans, like a whale song … No. That's all wrong. But it shows what I'm trying to get across. Words don't work. Language is inadequate. I know what I am saying because I have merged, I have communed and I have done it without the slightest recourse to language.

Professor Langeweile is the most interesting of the hundreds of people who have quizzed me since the revelation. He is quite enlightened, I think, and he truly wants to know, not to get an advancement, a promotion or something, but for himself, in order to understand. He has spent time in India, I think he said, and studied their mystics, and the Christian ones, and he says that is really what he sees in me. He is still stuck dealing with language, and is quite rational and that holds him back, but his questions are of a different sort. He is humble and gets excited when suddenly he sees something, or is explaining about Hildegard of Bingen or someone like that, a real professor, and then catches himself and laughs and says, "Well, of course you know that." Sometimes I do and sometimes I don't but I nod and we laugh together. The music of the spheres. Mystics. The thing is that I am not a mystic; I'm not seeing the face of God or anything of the sort. I merge but it's not a religious experience, or maybe you could say it is one of a different kind, a communion of sorts. Yeah, there is that problem with language again.

I won't try to explain to you how I do it. Nobody has ever learned to ride a bike by following instructions on paper. It's an action, not a theory. If you think you can sign up and in just eight easy lessons at a low low price of just, you too can, well, you are on the wrong channel. Being, not doing.

This is about birds. They know, they take off, they have the instinct, an inborn, inbred something. Maybe we used to have it too and just bred it out, or suppressed it or something. I'm not a scientist, a geneticist, any more than I am the fraud that so many would like me to be. I have gone beyond, mastered, allowed myself the freedom to go beyond the suppression.

It's so much easier not to talk. I just do.

Watch. I stretch them out.

Look. Yes. Up here, way up here. My weight does not matter.

Sometimes after the grilling and all the nonsense I put up with, I get away and soar. I clear my mind of everything and there is nothing but flight, movement, being one with the air, with moisture in the air, with sunshine. I am becoming more attuned to the differentiations in the air itself, not just velocity and pressure but the very molecules of moisture and air.

Maybe it was something like this for Noah, after the waters receded and he was no longer listening to squawks and breathing flatulence inside the ark, and after constantly wondering *will I really get through this no matter what He said, and soon they'll start dying off, and eating each other and if only I had a tiny little space, only for myself to stretch, to only hear myself,* and then yes, and there was hope, and he began thinking yes, I will see land again, and sometimes, just sometimes I feel what he felt, I can stretch out and not feel and smell anyone else in the world, it is just air, moisture, sunshine, me. I brush the tops of the trees and I want to break off a twig, to carry it somewhere to say, "Look, there is land, there is hope, there is growth and life," but then I don't. It is best not to break off anything living. I don't have to prove. It is enough that I know.

I have pains occasionally, sensations, twinges. With birds suddenly a top flyer will hold a wing a little askew and is less aggressive at the feeder. Then sometimes he comes back good as new, but sometimes you don't see him anymore. A black crow covers my mind with a wing and I don't breathe. Maybe it's not *can't* but it certainly is *don't*. My heart is weighed down by a smell of an unremitting wet emptiness. I've never belonged anywhere but now sense this will be short. Professor Langeweile says the mystics talk of a great light. I'd welcome a great light but it might be a great darkness on the horizon. No, it's not a physical ailment; I don't want a CAT scan or a pill. It's not depression.

Noah was trapped on that ark. A regret came, too, after the initial relief that unlike those who had not opened up, he was still standing and breathing. But because he was a favoured one, for him it was *Behold, a dove came back to him in the evening and in her mouth was a freshly plucked olive leaf.* No doves at my feeders, not a single olive leaf.

As I was saying, the problem is language. I've merged, moved to a new realm. But that means no one can help sort it out. I have a body, a mind and more. I'm still exploring. I'm on my own.

Saturday, 8th March 2014

That Awkward Moment

by Rachel Ambrose

I can't help but bite my nails when I hear Charlotte coming down the hall. She's been grumpy and quick–tempered ever since Blake and I started dating, and I've been trying to avoid her since my ability to Deal With Shit has absolutely flatlined (not that it ever had much of a pulse to begin with). But I've resolved to be in a good mood today. Blake and I are meeting by the river to have a picnic lunch, and I've bought a new dress, and I want another girl's opinion on how it looks.

"Charlotte?" I call bravely out into the hall. She opens her bedroom door and stands there, nose wrinkled like I'm secretly keeping a rat with diarrhea in here. "What do you think of this?" I ask, spinning slowly to show off the dress. It's a fit and flare in a pretty peach color with white lace around the neckline and the hem, and I'm planning on wearing a little white sweater on top.

She shrugs. "It's fine. You know you're a day late on your half of the rent check, right? It was due yesterday."

I'd actually forgotten in the excitement of choosing brie or camembert to bring with me on the picnic. "I'll write you that check tonight," I say, blushing despite myself. Blake's really gone to my head, I think dizzily. He's taken me out on six dates so far and all of them have been amazing and thoughtful. I'd think he was gay if he wasn't trying to get his hands down my pants at every opportunity. Today I thought to wear a dress to make that mission easier. His thoughtfulness is rubbing off on me.

Charlotte shakes her head. "Honestly, if I hadn't reminded you, you wouldn't have had any clue at all, would you?"

"I'm sorry!" I say. "It's just that things have been a bit of a whirlwind lately, you know, with Blake and all."

"Yeah," she replies, shaking her head. "Blake's a real gentleman, knows how to treat a girl right." She forces this out through gritted teeth, and her hands are visibly shaking.

It's then that I realize that she's been into Blake this entire time and never said anything. How could I have missed this fact? I feel like an idiot. "I'm sorry," I say again, but now I say it slower and softer, lingering over my remorse.

"Whatever," she says. "I'll be in my room, Claire, and I'd appreciate it if you could just slip that check under my door when you get the chance, after you're done being swept off your feet all afternoon." She slinks away and slams her door, and I stand there for a minute, feeling the cold chill of her departure. I grab a bottle of wine from Charlotte's wine rack in the living room, grab my purse and tiptoe out the front door. Now that I've stolen her man, I may as well keep going and steal her wine, too.

Sunday, 9th March 2014

Rory's Glory

by Gill Hoffs

I hum a theme tune I can't quite remember as I wait for the elevator, and remind myself to tell Jenny at the agency the flavoured condoms they gave me last week made my crotch smell like bubblegum. I'd even checked my pubes in case my client had forgotten to take his Juicy Fruit out before going down on me. I'd made it look like I was playing with myself, which made our 'date' pass faster than it usually does – another note to self: do NOT pretend to do that with clients who have problems with stamina.

Today I'm booked for a spring wedding, a posh one. The client's ex is marrying some nob with a title, so I've travelled through the night in the back of a limo, ready for a preparatory breakfast and champagne with Rory, my jilted host.

The lift arrives with the soft ping of a hidden bell, and I appreciate the plush pink carpet and wood panelling inside it, push 7, and listen to the hum of the machinery transporting me upwards, then stride through its open doors and along the corridor towards room 721. Lilies, minus their staining stamens, are arranged in an alcove opposite his door, and I revel in the opulence of my surroundings. Fresh flowers, Howson sketches in gilt frames on the wall – I'm particularly impressed by the Bosnian sketches – and carpet so thick my feet sink centimetres with every step. It's worth taking on a job so far away if it means luxury like this.

He opens the door and catches me sniffing the flowers' peppery perfume. I smile, straighten, hold his slender body close then let him carry my hatbox and overnight bag in. Then I strip.

After an hour of sucking, licking, fucking, and flicking, we're done. My lips have swollen nicely — why bother with collagen when a lengthy blowjob does the trick? — and Rory's lost the strained look on his face. Some of the lines are gone from the freckled skin round his eyes, long-lashed eyes the purply-blue of a five pound note. He runs me a bath, and kisses the nape of my neck as I clip my hair up to keep its straightened length free of suds. I don't have to fake the shiver he provokes.

I can tell he's not used to being a client instead of a lover, running me a bath, putting a towel to heat on the radiator for when I get out, asking if I'd like a cup of tea and a biscuit while I'm in there. It's nice. He's nice. So nice that when he calls me by my work-name I almost correct him with my real one.

We dress slowly, him in a grey morning suit complete with top hat and tails and platinum cufflinks in the shape of sea-turtles, both of which I have to wiggle through the silk shirt, and me in a summery mint-green frock and pale aquamarine leather boots. My hat's a monster, a giant creation of cream and blue and green with tiny silk hydrangeas and seed pearls swirled round with lace and a brim as wide as the rings of Saturn. No undies, but a thick velvety wrap to match the dress and I'm done. Well, I think I'm done, but then Rory says, "Hold still a sec," and fastens a single chain round my neck. I turn a little to look in the mirror by the door, to see what's pulling it down, and it's a pearl. Not a typical white one, either, but a purply-green rainbow one on a platinum chain.

"Thank you. It's beautiful."

I mean it.

"It suits you."

Dammit, I blush.

The bride is so happy. Her father walks her down the aisle, with a similar grin, and I can feel Rory's thigh tense beside mine and rub it to soothe him, but he slips his hand into mine and squeezes instead. I would lean my head on his shoulder, but the bastard hat's too big. The minister breezes through the service with a smile and barely a pause at the "speak now or forever hold their peace" bit, though Rory's hand clutches mine as if he might just stand up and offer an objection for the hell of it, or rather, for the hell of witnessing a woman he once – still? – loved marrying the man of her dreams.

When they kiss he surprises me by cupping my chin and turning to kiss me. Not a 'So there!' kiss for the benefit of those around us, either. A gentle smooch, just lips, as if I was her and he was her husband. As if we were in love.

We fling confetti in the churchyard, some landing on the couple, some on the daffodils and hyacinths bordering the path to the waiting horse and carriage. I notice the bride looking for Rory amongst the crowd, glancing at his face and tipping her head slightly as if to check he is alright. His arm is warm and welcome round my waist and from the corner of my eye I can see him smiling and nodding back. The photographer flashes the grey from the sky, over and over as if this is a horrible nightclub with only a strobe to perk up the party. She poses with her husband and innumerable lineups of relatives, squalling children, and friends, then passes through the medieval archway. Pause – flash flash flash – step up to the carriage – flash flash flash – helped up to her seat – flash flash flash – sit watching husband climb in – flash flash flash – snuggle together – flash flash flash – wave goodbye – flash flash flash. And … gone.

We shake hands with people in suits and their female companions, murmur variations on "The bride looked divine!" and edge towards the vintage double-deckers parked far away from naked trees and defecating pigeons in the gravel carpark. I stumble on the gravel, and Rory takes my arm to help. Even when we get to the bus, he doesn't let go. We're the first there, and instead of just sitting anywhere he leads me up the narrow stairs to the top deck, then gestures with his free hand to the front row.

"After you."

I haven't sat like this since I was a child. The view is terrific: weathered gravestones, clusters of daffodils, and the vivid blue of muscari stand out between ancient yew trees and neat stone paths winding through the shadow at the back of the church.

"She seemed very happy."

He nods, smiles a little, private smile.

"She is. They make a good couple."

"There's just us here. Would you like me to do anything to help … pass the time?" I want to say 'make you feel better' but I don't want him to know I can tell he's struggling despite the smiles. He's very good at looking happy when he isn't. I wonder if it's a natural gift or due to a depressing amount of practice.

"Yes." He takes my hat off, smoothes down the strands this inevitably ruffles, then instead of guiding my head down to his crotch puts his arm round my shoulders and pulls me into his side for a hug. "Thanks. I know this is just work for you, but I'm still glad you're here."

I lean right in, enjoying his lack of aftershave and the solid warmth of his body. I can't remember the last time a hug was just a hug.

I want to say that sometimes it isn't just work.

Sometimes I get paid for things or people I quite enjoy doing anyway. The money's a bonus that pays the bills and keeps me focussed on the future.

But I saw how he looked at the bride.

So I stick to "Me too," and keep my heart closed. At least for today.

Monday, 10th March 2014

Swoon

by Susan Tepper

I name this one Swoon. In the cupboard a jar of apricot jam that's down to the dregs. I pry open the lid. "Swoon will like this," I say, placing the sticky jar on the floor near my futon. When he doesn't come out right away, I start feeling jumpy. My arms start itching. What if something happened to the sleek white rat? Maybe the others, ordinary brown, were jealous of the silky albino hair. Maybe they castrated Swoon.

Lying down on the futon, I touch my balls carefully. That time in Bellevue – the first shock treatment. I woke up to some orderly squeezing my balls. Now I shake them to be sure they're still attached. Worrying about Swoon which starts me hiccupping. I get up to open the window then slam it shut. A TV doc said sudden loud noise can stop the hiccups. Not this time. Still no sign of the Kingly white rat; though some others, the regulars, huddle around the jam jar.

The boys at the brick elementary school, the new one I found the next town over – those little darlings, they would like Swoon. Those boys, they'll come out of hiding. One by one or in pairs. In their miniature GAP clothes just like the daddies wear. All I need to do is open the car door and in they'll climb. For Swoon. They'll get off the freaking jungle gym and all that other kiddie crap the schools install to keep them busy. Distracted. Too busy to notice a man in a car who watches their every movement. Loving them. Each of them. Whole lines of little darlings. My boys.

In an hour, when the recess starts, I'll be parked near the fence. Waiting with Swoon.

Tuesday, 11th March 2014

Shady Grace

by Jessica McHugh

Not a day passes that Edward McKenzie doesn't wish his mother, Betty, had died in the accident instead of Grandma Eleanor. She shouldn't have been driving anyway. Eleanor had offered to take the wheel, but as usual, his mother lashed out when her functionality was questioned. Betty McKenzie had screamed, jerked the wheel, gone mad at the wrong moment.

She'd also been the least harmed by the collision and shed the fewest tears over its result. Her lack of guilt made Edward hate her even more when she forced him to hear her confession. The vodka on her breath was louder than her regret, but he had to give her God's forgiveness. To this day, his own has never been offered.

His disgust at Betty isn't helped by the fact that she still lives in town, or that he visits the most abusive resident of Shady Grace Nursing Home every Tuesday. These visits are his penance. For one day a week, he takes the abuse so someone else doesn't have to.

"Hello, Betty."

His mother's head bobs, but she doesn't turn from the window. He sets a chair beside her and sits, touching her shoulder, but her gaze is fixed on the bare branches outside.

"How are you feeling today, Mom?"

"Eighty−seven in a shithole. Give me some room for Christ's sake. You're practically on top of me," she says, exhaling a cloud of liquor.

In spite of Shady Grace's no−alcohol policy, Edward isn't surprised. He doesn't know how her sour tongue sweet−talks the nurses out of searching her room, but after a lifetime with the woman, he suspects fear is involved.

As a child, Edward often pretended Betty was just some loud, mean dog who passed out on their couch or threw up on the dining room table. He also used the soft, sweet−smelling things in his grandmother's apartment for distraction. Wrapped in chiffon, he couldn't hear his mom's slurred insults or the ridicule from townspeople about the "drunk woman who killed her own mother."

But it doesn't work anymore. Even dressed as a man, Edward hears his fears blast from those in town. "Just look at his mother," he thinks they whisper. "Are you surprised he turned out to be a freak?"

Edward opens the top drawer of Betty's bureau. Beneath the clutter of letters and hairpins he finds a bottle of cheap rum. He takes it out and her head turns. Her eighty year−old body looks like a papier−mâché skeleton, but alcohol abuse has left a fatty shell sagging on her skull.

"Put the bottle back," she barks, her liquor−lard shaking.

"You're going to kill yourself with this stuff," Edward says, tucking the bottle into his jacket pocket.

"I've been hearing that since I was eleven. I guess it's not a very aggressive killer, huh?" she replies. "Or were you referring to my soul, *Father*?"

"Your soul is a lost cause, I'm afraid."

"You may be a priest, but I don't think you're anyone to judge on unsalvageable souls. Yours is the most perverted I've ever seen," Betty says. "You should thank your lucky stars no one but me knows how perverted."

Edward sighs. "I don't have any lucky stars anymore."

She sings a snide "boo hoo" and stands to face him. "You think I ever had any? With a pious mother and a freak for a son? What did I have to be thankful for, or be proud of?"

"I'm not going to apologize to you for anything."

"Why should you? You're no more to blame for your trip−ups than a retard on roller skates."

"Mom, that's horrible."

"Well, I'm a horrible person, aren't I? A lost cause?" she asks, her arms flapping like an injured bird. "You can drown your misery in your grandmother's perfume, why can't I drown mine in liquor?"

"You don't know anything about my misery, Betty. You never did."

"I think I know a bit," she says, grabbing her cane. Although she leans on it with each step, it isn't used for walking. No, not Mother's cane.

It taps the floor, a portentous metronome to pain, but Edward glares at Betty, unafraid. Her chins quiver in amusement before the cane rises. Betty's slower these days, but her arm hasn't lost its snap. Her cane strikes his thigh, but he doesn't give her the satisfaction of flinching. As the fiery stripe burns down his leg, Edwards clenches his jaw and swallows his pain. In the past, he might have run. He might have cried out or cursed at her, but none of those things ever made him feel better, and none ever taught her a lesson.

He lifts his chin, latches onto Betty's cane, and wrenches it from her hand. She scoffs, but there's shock behind the derision − for Edward, too. The shock turns to pride when he throws the cane to the floor and his mother backs away.

"Where's the rest?" he asks.

"I don't know what you mean."

He looks into the drawer, rifling the contents for more bottles. He doesn't find any, but something familiar catches his eye.

He removes the picture, his heart racing. The boy in the photo smiles, which means he hasn't been broken yet. He's still strong. All things are still possible. And with possibility at the helm, a strong child can change the world.

Betty slams the drawer closed, smashing Edward's fingers. Growling through the pain, he drops the photo to the floor. His mother kicks it under the bureau, hiding the strong child from the world again, and pulls a flask from her robe. After a smirking swig, she drops the flask in her pocket.

"Don't think a memento or two means anything," she says. "There's a lot of trash around here."

He walks to the door, whispering, "I know that, Mother." Massaging his throbbing hand, he feels small again – until he plucks her cane from the floor. If she doesn't need it to walk, she doesn't need it at all.

Edward McKenzie hooks the cane on his arm and closes the door on his mother, wishing it were closing forever. He says, "See you next Tuesday," but before the door shuts, he hopes the last thing Betty hears is the sound of him breaking her cane in half.

Rotted Leaves, Wilted Flowers

by Shane Simmons

Our heads hang silently as we brush aside rotted leaves and wilted flowers with our bare hands to reveal the two plaques. I peel the polythene wrap from a bunch of flowers I'd picked up on the way and arrange them into the empty pots at the side. "That looks nice," she comments.

The muddied plastic bags around our shoes rustle against the soggy grass as we stand back and I look at the engravings. I read the words to myself, over and over. Aunt Patricia sobs quietly. Should I have been doing the same? I gently pat her back, we say nothing.

Back at the cemetery path we untie the bags and place them in the bin. From the boot of her car, Aunt Patricia lifts a large, tartan picnic basket. "I know it's a little chilly, but I thought it would be nice to have something here." We sit down on a nearby bench. She pulls forth a flask of hot tea, perfectly quartered salmon and cream cheese sandwiches, and even a small Tupperware box of biscuits. There's nothing to break the silence except the birds and our own conversation.

"You don't look like you've been eating!" she scorns.

"I have, just all the wrong things and at the wrong times."

She sighs. "And how's work?"

"Oh, it's going well enough. How's Uncle John doing?"

"Looking forward to retirement, but they seem to want to keep him on as long as they can. It's a shame you won't be able to stay for dinner."

"I only managed to get a half–day off, we're on a tight deadline to get the image archive started online."

She pours more tea into the plastic cup in my hand and asks, "Do you miss them?"

I rub my curled fingers past my closed lips, only knowing that I should say, "Yes."

"I have a little something for you in the car. You will let me drop you off at your work when we're done here?"

"But aunty, it's such a long ..."

She tuts and shakes her head before she shushes me. "I insist, it'll be nice."

A spot of drizzle lands just on my cheek. "We'd better pack this all up soon, those clouds look ominous."

My phone vibrates against my thigh, I'd left it on silent since the cemetery.

"Hey hun," I hear her voicemail, "I know it's a hard day for you, hope you're OK. Say 'hello' to your lovely aunt and uncle, call me later if you like."

"Who's that?" Aunt Patricia asks.

"It's Sandra," I say, slipping my phone back into my pocket, "she says hello. I don't think she's drunk, as yet." Aunt Patricia guffaws. I don't think she'll soon forget Sandra, who tagged along with me for my Boxing Day visit, drank far too much mulled punch, crushed a bed of winter pansies when she fell on them before violently throwing up into a box hedge. It took a fair while to hose that multi–coloured mess away.

"So, aside from boisterous Sandra, have you met anyone, someone special?" Aunt Patricia enquires from the steering wheel. "Just, I want you to know that if there is anyone, anyone at all, they're as welcome to visit as you are."

She of course means well, so I give a simple "Thank you" in response. But there is no one.

As she drives us towards the city, Classical FM plays second fiddle to the hiss of tyres against damp tarmac. The roads become harder to see through waves of lashing rain. The traffic slows to a crawl along the A20. But it's good to spend some more time with her.

Eventually, we pull up outside of my work. Aunt Patricia leans over to open the glove compartment, she takes out a bag and hands it to me.

"I found this photo. It was taken when your mum and dad first started dating. I had a copy framed for you."

I unwrap the white tissue paper to find a pair of faces staring back at me from inside a silver filigree frame. They're young, at ease, and dare I say, happy. They're strangers to me. I look at it, a beautiful, beaming woman resting her head upon the shoulder of the handsome, youthful man next to her. I don't recognise them.

"It was taken at Margate. It was a gorgeous summer's day, a Sunday if I remember right. All four of us jumped on a train together and went to the coast. It was so busy. I can recall it like yesterday." Her voice crackles and as I turn to look at her I see her eyes are fogged over.

"Thank you aunty, it's a lovely picture." I fold the tissue paper back over the frame and lean across to give her a hug. "I promise to come over sooner, perhaps this weekend?" But the words muffle against her shoulder.

She whispers into my ear, "Please don't forget them." When she pulls away from my hug, I see her eyes are now red and as swollen as a riverbank about to burst.

"I'd better get going," I say. "Thank you so much for the lift, tell Uncle John I was asking after him. I'll call tonight to make sure you got home safely."

I clamber out of the car, and quickly disappear into the building. The bag in my hand trembling, I stop dead in the foyer to take slow, deep breaths. I wipe my eyes clear. I'm grateful there's no one around.

Somehow, she must've known I had almost forgotten them.

Thursday, 13th March 2014

Canary

by Michelle Elvy

Stevie's riding his bicycle. It's early March and it's snowing. He hasn't ridden much this year. He only pulled it last week from its musty place in the garage, leaning against the old ping pong table no one uses any more. He used to ride it everywhere – every day after school, every weekend. All over the roads of South County, getting lost in the dark narrow spaces that curved and bent in unexpected ways. He could ride those roads blindfolded. He knew every single moss‒covered bank and every single turn.

But February was unusually cold, and January – well, January was lost. And last summer he only rode it once. Most days last summer, he was with Manny, Rick, and Lucky. He'd known Manny since they were eight, when Manny's family had moved in two doors down. Rick lived closer to town, so they didn't see him as often, but Rick was tedious anyway, even if he was Manny's cousin. Lucky, on the other hand, became a permanent fixture in their lives in sixth grade – the coolest kid by far, without even knowing it, which is what made him so cool – and he and Manny and Stevie were near inseparable ever since. They moved from collecting Pokemon to playing Mindcraft together as their tastes morphed over the years. Why they started jacking cars was something they couldn't explain; it was outrageous – a challenge and a thrill. And no one expected it from them, so they got away with it. Stevie's got a knack for breaking into cars, you could say. But it's all harmless fun — they'd take a short joyride then ditch the car, sometimes only two streets from where they jacked it. It is in fact the only dysfunctional thing about Stevie, really, his only vice. He doesn't drink and he doesn't get stoned with Lucky and Rick. Stevie's a good student, a good son.

Now he's riding down Claret Street, back behind the old post office, not entirely sure where he's going. It just feels good, with the snow falling lightly on his face, with his fingers gripping the handlebars in the morning chill.

Up ahead he sees a small girl on the side of the road. As he gets closer he sees she has no coat. Wait, no: she's wearing her pajamas. He slows and he sees that she's barefoot. Her long hair is hanging over her face, her bangs covering her eyes. She's just standing there. Her pajamas have small cats on them — cats chasing mice. When he stops in front of her she looks up and he sees it's Sylvie, Ellie's little sister. She's easily a half—mile from home, just standing there on the road, with her head down.

"Sylvie?"

No answer. Not a muscle moves.

"Sylvie? Are you alright?"

"I lost my bird."

"Your bird?"

"His name is Yellow Bird. Like Big Bird."

"Where'd you lose him?"

"Out here. He flew out the window and I followed him."

"Did you find him?"

"No."

"Do you want a ride home?"

"No. I have to keep looking."

Stevie shifts on his seat. He's not sure what to do, but he's pretty sure he ought to find a way to get Sylvie home.

"You want me to help you look?"

"Yes."

"Alright. So let's walk back the way you came, and we'll look out for him as we go. Sometimes birds fly back to their homes, you know." He doesn't think this is true, but it seems like a good thing to say.

"I don't think that's true, but OK," says Sylvie.

Stevie hops off his bike and they start walking back toward Sylvie's road. They are both pretty wet now; it's just warm enough to make the snow melt as it floats down to earth. It will all turn to ice tonight but for now it's just slushy. There are puddles in the potholes and Stevie guides Sylvie away each time they get near one. She's maybe four or five, he can't tell. She's barefoot and wet from the falling snow and he's worried more about her fingers and toes than her bird. "What are all those stickers for?" asks Sylvie, pointing to the frame of Stevie's bike. He tells her about some of them – one from Vermont, one from Maine, one from Illinois. Many, many stickers. All from different family trips.

"I like the bear," says Sylvie. "And the smiling sun." California. And the sunshine state. Both very far from here.

Stevie's had the Schwinn since he was twelve. It's old-fashioned, sure – not a BMX, not an offroad machine – but it's the bike his dad got him for Christmas that year – *just like my old bike*, his dad said – and he likes it for that reason alone. All around him his friends have rebelled more and more: Lucky in a constant cloud of weed, Manny practically dropping out of school. But besides stealing an occasional Honda hatchback, Stevie is still a contented part of society and his family. He tolerates his little brother more than is warranted, and he likes his parents. He feels he's a bit too bland, but it's a terrible truth he can't help. He's just not a bad boy.

When they turn onto Sylvie's road – the old gravel road – they avoid the big pothole at the edge and move more toward the center. And there, lying only a few feet away, Stevie sees a small brownish pile with sticky feathers and a sad pale yellow showing through the wet mass, like little bits of hay. Stevie keeps walking. A mild panic grips him and he wants to run. He hopes that his body and his bike are blocking the view just enough so Sylvie does not see. But just as they are almost past the pothole and moving on toward Sylvie's driveway – which he can see up ahead, only a few more houses down the street – a truck turns into the road behind them, and Sylvie pivots to see it. She waves at the driver, her neighbor, then somehow catches the yellow smudge out of the corner of her eye, and Stevie knows there's no avoiding it. He braces himself for inevitable wailing. He feels certain Sylvie will need to be carried the rest of the way and he briefly wonders how he'll carry her and his bike and the dead bird.

Instead, Sylvie takes his hand and says, "Look. There's Yellow Bird. In the big puddle."

"I see him." The only thing Stevie can think to say.

"I have to help him out."

"Yeah."

"You have to help me."

"Yeah."

Stevie rests his bike on the side of the road and digs in his backpack and finds a blue–checkered handkerchief. He pulls it out, smooths a used crinkly corner on his knee, and hands it to Sylvie.

"Here."

Sylvie takes the handkerchief from him and blows her nose loudly. Then she steps toward the large pothole and reaches out toward Yellow Bird. She can't quite reach him, though, and Stevie thinks she may fall forward and into the puddle. He steps quickly to her side, kneels in the gravel beside her. He scoops up the dirty mess in his hands. He looks at Sylvie, who has now spread the hanky in her palms. She's holding them out with an expectant look. For a moment, Stevie almost laughs at the scene – this unlikely calm child with her outstretched hands, caring for a bird so quietly while the cat and mouse scream around in maddening circles all over her now soaking wet pajamas, her bare toes poking out red with cold and her nose running steadily down to her upper lip. He places the bird in her palms and watches as she gingerly folds the corners of the hanky over her bird.

"You're gonna help me bury him, aren't you." It's not really a question.

They stand. Stevie pulls his bike up by the handlebars and they walk down the road together toward Sylvie's house. He's thinking about this brave girl with the crazy cat pajamas and it suddenly dawns on him that he has not thought about Ellie once during this whole episode – Ellie who almost incessantly rattles his thoughts; Ellie who has not seen him in a month, not since Lucky's funeral; Ellie who he's sure is as lost as he is; Ellie who may not even know he exists anymore. And now he's walking toward her house.

His throat feels a hard lump.

"Come on," says the cat–mouse–bird girl. "Yellow Bird will need a good funeral. With songs. Do you sing? Ellie will sing."

Now he has a new image of Ellie: Ellie, who sings.

Trail's End

by Len Kuntz

It's noon on a Friday and already the liquor store is packed.

I ask a man wearing a hunter's tartan shirt, "What's the deal? Why's it so busy?"

He looks at me, then walks away without a word, as if I've offended him, as if I'm foul–smelling.

The clerk at the counter wears a turban. He seems annoyed but has beautiful skin, shiny, too, the color of maple syrup.

My cart is filled with five gallons of gin and loads of tonic. When I ask if they sell limes, Turban Head flares his nostrils and says, "This isn't a grocery store."

I feel like punching him. I feel like strangling him with his turban and watching that pretty skin of his turn blue, then purple, but there's a woman in line behind me whose Chihuahua keeps trying to hump my leg.

"Really, lady? Can't you get your damn dog fixed?"

"Fix yourself," she says, not doing anything about the filthy mongrel.

When Turban Head flashes me a grin, I flip him off.

My next stop is a convenience store where I buy cigarettes. I haven't smoked since high school. I open the pack and light up as soon as I exit the place. It's the same as if I've shoved a blow torch down my throat and no matter how subtly I inhale, I end up hacking.

Around the corner, on the curb by a dumpster, two teenagers are singing a Dylan song, *Blowin' in the Wind*, the guy strumming a guitar.

They notice me but don't say anything. The girl is blonde and pale and her partner has dreadlocks coiled all over his head like hydras made out of yarn.

When they're finished, the girl asks if they can hitch a ride. I tell them I'm not going their way. They ask how I know. I say because I don't know where I'm going. The guy says, "That's cool. We're just floating, too."

"My car's loaded with stuff."

The guy tugs at his shirt. "Look at us, man, we're skinny."

They are. A pair of ragamuffins.

"All right," I say. "If you can fit, you're in."

I've got the gin on the front seat. The trunk and back seat are loaded with shit I don't really remember buying, and I only took it because I'm never going back to the lake house again.

"See?"

"No sweat, man," the guy says. He lifts up the sacks of gin, sits down, pats his lap and has his girl sit on him.

"I think that's maybe illegal," I say.

"Lighten up," the guy says. "I'm Buddy. This is Lana."

They keep singing in the car, going through Dylan's early protest catalog. I've been driving for half an hour when I remember the guy's guitar. "Where is it?" I ask.

"Left it," Buddy says.

"You left it back there?"

"It wasn't mine anyway, plus it's a piece of crap."

Near Seattle, a torrent begins, but they don't stop singing. Now it's *Hurricane*.

I wonder how they know such old songs. I wonder where their parents are and what the hell they're doing, but I don't ask because learning too much about people has only caused me trouble. But it feels good to have company, even if they're more strange than strangers.

It's night by the time I reach the Idaho border and I'm beat, so I pull over at Trail's End Motor Lodge.

Buddy says, "Hey, man, you mind if we crash with you? Just for tonight. We'll sleep on the floor."

When I tell them that sounds like a bad idea, Buddy pulls out a blunt as large as a cigar. "We could party," he says.

In the room, I go through half a gallon of gin like it's a scorching day and I'm drinking lemonade. Buddy and Lana are blitzed, sitting with their backs against the wall. Buddy keeps tracing patterns on Lana's face, then marveling over his designs, as if his fingertips are leaving paint, which has me thinking their pot must be laced with something.

He tells her she's beautiful. He compares her to springtime, a wild fawn. He goes on and on. Lana stares back at him, her eyes wet. She unbuttons his shirt, helps him off with his jeans.

"Hey," I say. "No way."

Lana pulls her ratty sweater off. She's braless. In the time it takes me to polish off my glass, she's naked and they're both entwined, rubbing as if trying to light a fire with their flesh. I think about throwing a bottle against the wall to make them snap out of it. I think about Virginia and how different it felt with her, me wanting nothing than to please her.

I watch Buddy and Lana writhe and slide. I listen to them whimper and whisper. I tell myself this is just a movie I'm watching, that I'm merely a spectator, that all this is as right as rain.

Saturday, 15th March 2014

Third Inning

by Michael Webb

The tumblers of thought click into place as I walk across the diamond in the Florida sun, sweating pleasantly while the crowd buzzes around me. The events of the previous inning, a long home run from our second baseman Juan Mihares followed by a fastball right between the threes on the back of the uniform of our right fielder 'Sliding' Billy Hamilton, suddenly spelled it all out for me. I have to hit somebody, and the first man up in the fourth, Marlon Starling, is, in baseball's peculiar calculus, the equivalent player.

It is one of the rules. When they get one of yours, you get one of theirs. It's Sean Connery logic, from his speech on the bridge in the film *The Untouchables*. "That's the Chicago Way!" Efficient and brutal, it is the way pitchers, long isolated because of our peculiar work schedules and fragility like hothouse flowers, prove we are part of the team, by stepping up and defending our mates the only way we can, an equal and opposite fastball in the ribs.

Hitting batters is rude in the extended casual attitudes of the spring. Results don't matter, a sudden run of success or paralyzing failure greeted with the same casual bromide, "it's just spring training." Plunking, or dusting, or flipping someone, or throwing what they called a purpose pitch, is something you reserve for the more serious combat of the regular season, when jobs and careers and the agate type that determine our value for all time is determined.

It was determined before the game that the fourth inning is mine, for good or ill, so I just headed out without being told anything. I'm confident my spot on the team is secure, but just like everyone else, I have to get my work in, and a quick inning will no doubt raise my stock in the minds of my new bosses, which can't hurt. But the reality of the situation has suddenly come to me. I think about Charlie Brown, and I feel a stab of stomach pain.

I'm at the mound, Hector Cruz, our catcher, already there with the baseball.

"OK, 1 for heat, 2 for slide, 3 for change?" he says in thick, accented English. We have spoken a few times, but I have thrown only a couple of times to the man who will receive the majority of my deliveries this year.

"Yup," I say.

"We flipping this fucker?"

I put my glove to my lips, a pointless gesture intended to thwart HD−watching lip readers. I hate throwing at anyone. It is against my nature, and everyone who does this for a living knows the names, the unwary or unlucky who were hit in the head or the face, ending a career, or back in 1920, the life of Cleveland's Ray Chapman. In such a precise matter, where fractions of inches change destinies in fractions of seconds, a mistake, though unlucky, is not far from the minds of anyone.

I think about my new teammates, wary in a workplace where friends are shipped to Toronto or San Diego or Columbus without another word. I feel their eyes on me. Does this guy have any balls? Will he defend me if I'm the one who gets whacked? Will positive feelings toward me help an outfielder dive for a dying quail? Will it coax a walk to extend a rally and get back a run for me?

I think about baseball, its codes and traditions, and of Starling, staring at me from the on−deck circle, having done nothing but share a uniform with someone who could have simply made a dumb mistake under the sweaty light in God's waiting room. I don't want to hurt him. I don't want to hurt anyone. I think I remember reading that Starling is a new father, a baby boy born over the winter, according to the note on ESPN.com.

But I have a family to feed too. I have new teammates whose doubts I have to soothe. There are rules, and I'm their prisoner. I take the ball from Cruz' enormous mitt.

"Yup," I say.

Petals and Perfume

by James Claffey

The twenty chickens sell at market for a not too shabby profit, given the amount of feed the Bird had invested in that winter. A bitter, miserable time, too, it was. The nights short as burned candles on saucers, the rain never less than drizzling down for weeks at a time. The money burns a hole in the Bird's pocket, so he steps in to Quinn the Haberdasher's.

"D'you have a pair of those fancy slippers with the fleece lining?" he asks, patting his oil−slick hair down.

"Grand day to you too, Bird," Quinn replies. "Are you looking for the ones from Australia?" He slips behind a shelled curtain and returns with an opened shoebox.

"No, no. Not those ones. The ones with the curled up toes. Like feckin' genies wear, you know?"

"We don't have the like. Sure, won't you take these anyway? They're your size and all."

"I'd rather get a new frying pan, instead, thanks all the same." And out the door he marches, coat whipping in the wind, his face lashed by the stingers of rain pelting down from the dark sky. Instead of more shopping he steps into the arcade and plugs a few coins in the slot machine. He has a terrible love for the one−armed bandits, and imagines a holiday to Las Vegas one day, to Caesar's Palace. He hears they have doormen with white gloves, and moving statues. It'd be powerful fun to play the machines there, he thinks. Maybe he'll do a bit of partying while he's at it.

Across from him, the Hanlon boy rides a pinball machine, his crotch banging the front of it, a high−pitched whine coming from the screen when he sets the steel ball on its journey. The lad would be better served doing his bloody homework if he was worth his salt, the Bird thinks. Cherries aligned and jingled coins fall into the tin tray. It's turning out to be some day.

In Lowery's Pub the bell above the door clangs and Ned Lowery nods. "Greetings and salutations!"

The Bird orders a Guinness and Powers and stands Ned a drink.

"Your health," Ned says, raising the glass.

"Slainte." He drains the warm Guinness in one go, imagining there'll be nothing but bloody Budweiser beer in Las Vegas. Behind the bar a calendar for Russian Vodka a good two months off the mark, the young lass all skin and lipstick in a skimpy Santa Claus outfit, a white stole across her bare breasts.

"She's hot on her leather," the Bird remarks, knocking on the bar to signal time for another.

"She's a grand sight, and make no mistake. Look at those plump lips, and isn't it a shame we've no young ones like her in this town?"

At the far end of the counter a woman wrapped in a dull shawl worries her toenails with silver clippers, the occasional click causing the Bird to flinch, afraid the shards will land in his drink. She has a visible sadness to her, and he recognizes her as one of the travelers from the crossroads on the Navan Road, the ones he passes every week on the way to market. His cheeks flush when she catches him staring, but she shoots him a gap−toothed smile, and digs the dirt from under a big toe.

He drains the whiskey and raps the bar with his knuckles in farewell. With a bit of luck the tinkers will be gone by summer and he'll be off in America on the pig's back.

§

On the Dublin road the Bird tacks into the wind and his bicycle creaks along as the land−locked seagulls caw caw caw overhead. As he's freewheeling around the curve of the road toward home, a battered VW Camper van overtakes him, horn tooting, and a waving hand raised. The van pulls to the curb and the Bird sees it's the French woman from Hogan's bar. The one with the flute.

"Bird! How are you? Very windy, no?" She smiles, her hair ablow in the breeze.

"Ah, it's yourself. Nice to see you again." The Bird clears his throat and fiddles with the bell on the handlebar. "Fresh day, isn't it?"

"What is it about you Irishmen and the weather?" she asks, a hand smoothing down her grey hair. "Is it the only subject you are comfortable having an opinion about?"

"No, no. We'll talk the hind legs off a donkey if you give us a chance," he replies.

"Let us take the chance and drink some tea, then," Melodie says, and points at the small café across the road. "Shall we take tea over there?"

"Well, now. If you don't mind, I'd be happier if we took tea around the corner at my house, it that's all right with you?" The Bird dismounts his bike in anticipation and when she nods, he pushes the black Raleigh onto the footpath.

He puts the key in the latch and pushes the door inward, wheeling the bike into the hall and resting it on a long, white painted radiator. She follows him along the hallway, shutting the door behind her. The place is lit by bare electric bulbs, no shades over any of the lights, and wallpaper that curls from the walls.

"Sit down, now," he says, offering her the one empty chair at the kitchen table. The others are piled with newspapers and cardboard boxes.

"Are you moving out?" Melodie asks.

"Ah, no. It's the parents' bits and pieces. They both died in the last while and I'm getting through their belongings."

The whistling kettle startles Melodie and she says something in French, but the Bird only smiles and thinks how wonderful the strange words sound in her soft voice. Scald the pot. Three heaped spoons of black tea. Jug of milk from the fridge. The Bird takes a packet of Marietta biscuits from the cupboard and fans them in a semi−circle on a plate.

In silence they sit, the ticking of the clock punctuating the sips of tea, the crunch of biscuit, and when the Bird tries to say something he chokes on a crumb, his face reddening. Melodie slaps him on the back with the palm of her hand. He rises, the chair rattling to the floor, and coughs violently, a spatter of wet crumbs spraying the air. Melodie rights the chair and rubs the Bird's back, her hand gentle and comforting to him.

"You must think I'm an awful eejit," he says, sitting back down and finally catching his breath.

"Oh, no. You are a nice man. This happens to me too sometimes." Melodie smiles at him over her raised teacup.

"Would you like to see the rest of the house?" he asks, rising from his chair and gesturing towards the hallway.

"Oui, I mean, yes, of course."

He walks behind her to the front room, her dress flowery, reds, greens, yellows, a meadow of movement, a sea of memory. He closes his eyes, imagining the skin beneath the cotton, the softness. All he hears though is his mother's voice admonishing him to get a hold of himself, and why on earth would a woman like this French harlot ever see anything in him.

"Shut up!" He claps a hand to his mouth, and says, "Sorry. I was talking to my mother."

"But, she is dead. No?" Melodie stops at the door to the front room.

"Yes, but I hear her voice in my head."

The French woman smiles, reaches for the Bird's hands, parts the flowers of her dress and engulfs him in a cascade of petals and perfume.

Monday, 17ᵗʰ March 2014

The Lucky Ones

by Gwendolyn Joyce Mintz

It's St. Paddy's Day and, being restaurant workers, Mora and
Aaron can't get the night off. Aaron makes Mora promise to
make Diane promise that she'll show up for the March meeting
of "The Suicide Club."

"The guys are so new," he tells Mora about Phil and
Vincent. "I don't want them to think we don't care about their
pending deaths."

So Diane shows.

Kelly's, the bar and grill where they've been meeting, is
hopping. Full of revelers dressed in green, conversations spiced
with a touch of brogue.

Diane waits at the hostess podium, her arms crossed tight.
She's aware of the dulling sensation building inside.

The hostess appears. "Booth or the table?"

Diane shakes her head. "You know, I think I'll wait for the
others and see what they want." She takes a seat on the bench by
the door.

At the appointed time, Vincent walks through the door,
followed by Phil with the left leg he seems to drag along.

Diane pops up and approaches them before the hostess can.
"It's really crowded in here," she says. "And loud." She raises
her voice for emphasis.

Vincent looks around. "Not meeting then?"

"We can go somewhere else," she says.

Vincent glances at Phil who shrugs.

Diane takes it as a 'yes' and she leads them to the door.

"Another time?" the hostess asks.

Diane looks back over her shoulder. "Yeah, sure," she says.

They opt for a diner. A booth. Diane on one side, Vincent and Phil on the other.

"So, you couldn't take all their happiness?"

Diane looks up from her coffee cup at Vincent. It only takes a moment for her to register what he meant. "They're not happy; they're *drunk*." She holds his gaze until he looks away. Shaking her head slightly, she turns her attention back to her cup. She wants to tell him that they're the lucky ones; that the closer they get to death, the closer they are to what matters.

"So what exactly do we do at these meetings?" Phil asks, cutting into her thoughts.

"We really haven't done anything yet," she replies. "I think we're just gonna have a place to go talk."

"I still can't believe you want to kill yourself," he continues.

Diane's smile is wry. "Well, if I could find someone to do it for me ..." She sips at the coffee. Lowering the cup, she asks; "So what's your story?"

Phil lifts his useless left hand. "Cerebral palsy. So tired of living with it."

"Tired. That's what this singer said in her suicide note. She was tired."

Vince jumps into the conversation. "And your method will be?"

"Pills. This time," Diane shares, "I'm opting for pills. Just like Marilyn Monroe."

Phil agrees that's how he'll go. "It's not like I could tie a rope or something."

They all chuckle.

"For me," Vincent says when their laughter subsides, "it's gonna be a bang."

Something inside tells Diane to keep quiet but she can't. "I don't buy what people say about suicide being selfish, well it is if you're leaving children behind and if you shot yourself. That's pretty selfish."

Vincent scowls.

"You leave a mess that someone else has to clean up. How is that fair?"

"Exactly," Phil chimes in. "I've always thought Hemingway was a jerk for making his wife find him that way."

Vincent glares at Phil. Turning back, he lifts his glass to his lips and finishes off his soda. He sets it down and says, "You're both full of shit."

Phil laughs.

Diane looks across the table though Vincent is now busy reading the copy on the placemat.

She's gonna tell Mora to tell Aaron that they need some kind of rules if they're going to keep meeting.

Diane thought she was going to like Vincent. Now she's having spiteful thoughts about him. She plans, now, to cut this evening short before her feelings escalate. After all, they're meeting to work out killing themselves, not each other.

Tuesday, 18th March 2014

The Comedian

by Stephen V. Ramey

I'm in the produce section of the supermarket closest to our house. Anne needs green peppers for tonight's dinner. It's only noon, but I couldn't stand being in the house any longer. When I get stuck on writing a scene, I soon find myself feeling the cancer inside, pushing at my rectum, spreading through my blood like dandelion fluff.

Staccato laughter draws my attention. Jimmy Magerko is holding court near the cantaloupe bins, a half—dozen shoppers arrayed in a semi—circle. I should be surprised, but nothing surprises me where Jimmy is concerned.

"Don't get me wrong," he's saying. "I love my honey, but really? Another stray? You can't drop a crumb in our house without starting a catfight. I told her she could take in another one the day she lets me have a threesome." He dons his go—to expression, part smug defiance, part innocent kid caught with one hand in the cookie jar. "The new cat's name is Fluffy." Polite laughter. "And, yeah, I got my *ménage a trois*. I have the claw marks to prove it." Louder laughter and an actual guffaw.

A uniformed man approaches him. "I'm sorry, sir, but you'll need to move along. No solicitation."

Jimmy's eyes flash, a striking effect when combined with his hawkish profile and sleek silver hair. "Do I look like I'm soliciting? Did I tell these good people that I'm appearing this weekend at Benefields?" He does a deadpan to an elderly woman hunched over her shopping card. "That's in the Mill Street building, darling. They have a ramp." I wince, but the woman only chuckles. Jimmy is always saying that comedy is an equal opportunity offender, and everyone is the butt of one joke or another.

The shoppers disperse, leaving the uniformed man to confront Jimmy. Jimmy hands him a cantaloupe, and walks toward me.

"What did you think?" he says.

"I only heard the last joke," I say. "It was good."

"Thanks. It's always best to include a kernel of truth."

"Which part, the cat or the threesome?"

Jimmy winks. "Does a magician give away his tricks?"

I look around. "Where's Rose? I thought she was recording your routines for a webcast."

"She is. I'm just testing new material for my pop–up at Lowe's tonight. Come on over if you have time. I hear they sell tomatoes in case I bomb. Well, tomato plants."

"I don't think we can make it," I say. "Anne has a meeting after dinner."

"Come without her. Do you need a ride?"

"No," I say. Sadness wells up suddenly. "I'm ... I need some alone time, you know?"

"Sure," Jimmy says. "There will be other gigs." He touches my forearm. "Did you get your results back, is that what's bugging you?" The intensity of that gaze serves his comedy well, but makes friendship a little dodgy at times. I feel as if I'm being sized up for a meal.

"Not good," I say. I didn't see a specialist, but Dr. D did convince me to come in for a follow–up exam. More blood work, a CAT scan, and the diagnosis is clearer. I have growths in my lower GI, a suspicious spot on my liver. It doesn't look good for the good guy.

"What's next?" Jimmy says.

"Nothing," I say. "I'm done with doctors."

"I don't get you, man, you're going to stand by and let that shit eat you up? What about Anne? Don't you care what happens to her?"

"Of course I do. That's one reason I'm doing this, Jimmy. I don't want to put her in the poor house."

"You have insurance. I heard Anne tell Rose."

"Yeah, but it's only bronze. High deductible, high out of pocket. A week in the hospital, and our savings will be gone."

"That's bullshit," Jimmy says. "What are you really afraid of?"

"I'm not afraid. It's ..." I pick up an orange and rotate it in my hands. "I'm working on a book. I haven't told Anne yet because, well, because the last three books didn't get finished, but this is the one. I know it."

"Good for you," Jimmy says.

"If I start treatment, that'll be the end. I watched my dad go through surgery, radiation, chemo. Once you begin, it takes over your life. I can't afford that now."

Jimmy gives a sour look. "Seems to me that if you watched your dad die, you ought to be a little less enthusiastic about following that same road."

The security guy interrupts, still holding the cantaloupe. "You need to move along, sir." He nudges Jimmy. Jimmy nudges back. Several bunches of bananas fall. The uniformed guy scrambles to pick them up.

Jimmy grabs my arm, and guides me to the next aisle. Bags of potatoes and onions surround us. I think of the earth they were pulled from, my father's grave.

"I don't want to die, Jimmy, I don't. There's only two things I've ever really wanted, to play professional baseball – took me seventeen years to figure out that was a pipe dream – and to write a book that matters, you know, like Tolkien or Salinger, something that leaves a mark."

"How about *Dianetics?*" Jimmy snorts. "That shit is so fucked up it's definitely going to leave a mark."

"I'm serious, Jimmy."

"And I'm not? Look, here's the thing — and, by the way, I'm a little disappointed that getting laid didn't make your top two goals, or having a great comedic friend for that matter — but this is the thing: we don't always get what we want, Stephen. Life is struggle, man. Take me, for example. Some nights the audience is so dead it would make Brad Pitt nervous. Do I give up? Hell, no, I dig deeper next time."

"Yeah, well writing a novel is not the same thing."

The security guy shows up again. He looks determined this time, steely eyes, mouth set, hand hovering by his hip as if he's about to draw from a nonexistent holster. "You need to take it outside, gentlemen."

"Don't say anything to Rose," I say. "Anne talks to Rose at least twice a week."

Jimmy laughs. "Yeah, I'm going to start lying to my fourth wife, it worked so well for the first three."

"Sir —"

"Yeah, yeah," Jimmy says, brushing the security guy aside.

"I mean it, Jimmy. Anne can't find out. Not yet. She'll ... I don't know what she'll do. She trusts me, you know? We tell each other everything."

"Then tell her this," Jimmy says. "I know a bit about slippery slopes." He glances at the security guy, who is fumbling with a hand-held radio. "Try the green button, buddy."

Static sounds. The guy grins, triumphant.

"Okay, okay," Jimmy says. "I'm going." He walks briskly toward the exit. The security guy hangs back as if debating whether to kick me out too.

"Don't worry," I say. "Comedy's not contagious." I stroll to the chiller to pick a pack of peppers.

§

Anne is sitting at the kitchen table eating a salad when I walk through the back door. A half–dozen bottles of dressing are arranged before her. She has a habit of getting them all out even when she's eating alone. I usually end up putting them away. I shouldn't resent that – she's the one bringing home a paycheck these days – but I can't help myself. Why six, when you'll only use one?

"Would you like some green pepper?" I say, thrusting the plastic shopping bag forward.

She slides a cell phone across the table. My gut goes cold. I check my pocket. Yep, it's mine. Anne doesn't like it when I forget to take my phone with me. How will she reach me in an emergency?

"Sorry." I set the bag on the counter. "I guess I forgot."

"You have a voicemail," she says.

"Oh?"

"Doctor D'Orenzio."

Oh. "I wonder why –"

"She scheduled an appointment for you with Dr. Matta a week from Friday."

Damn. I smile sheepishly. "Yeah, I forgot to tell you. She wants me –"

"I Googled him," Anne says. "He's an oncologist."

"Yeah," I say, thoughts spinning. "It's, I'm, yeah, I'm writing a book. Survival rates for cancer. Dr. D –"

"Don't even bother making something up," Anne says. "You're a terrible liar." Her eyes gleam.

"No, really, I'm wri –"

"I could understand you hiding an affair," she says, "but *this*? Christ, Stephen, will I never get through to you? I'm your fucking wife! You don't have to hide behind your walls any more. You promised me, you ... promised."

"I know," I mumble. I promised to tear down the walls between us that had frustrated her so thoroughly before we married. *No secrets, Stephen. We'll build a bridge, we'll fight for each other.* "I'm sorry."

Her face suddenly balls up. She shoves her plate away, stands, and runs out of the room. I feel powerless as the plate balances on the table's edge like a roller coaster car reaching the top of a hill ... then topples. Salad splashes the floor, leaves glistening with oil.

I watch, open-mouthed, unable to articulate my thoughts. My feelings are clear enough, though. Guilt. Regret. If only I had acted faster, I might have stopped it all.

Father and Son

by Gay Degani

As the sun's orange glow streaks his window, Gus German watches the last few minutes of the TV news, Gracie alert at his feet, tail whisking across the shag carpet. He ignores the dog because he's learned that making any movement or comment at this time of day will send the animal into paroxysms of impatience. When the perky blonde newscaster finally signs off, the old man clicks off the TV and grins at his mutt. "You ready for your walk?"

The path down to the creek is steep, so the old man and the dog take their time, Gracie burying her muzzle in every clump of weeds, every pile of dirt. Boy Scouts have spent hours of community service cleaning up the mess from the January windstorm, all except for the huge eucalyptus that fell over Gus' favorite path. Each afternoon he and Gracie hope that when they reach that point, the tree will have been removed and they can go into the little clearing where the city recedes behind rustling shrubs, where chittering squirrels and afternoon parrots provide the only sounds. Gus longs for his Iowa roots, the serenity that comes from acres of endless corn around a stand of cedars, the burble of a stream.

He stops at the fallen eucalyptus, his closed mouth moving in silent frustration. What did he expect? Mounds of debris still wait for city pick—up at curbs along the Old Road.

Gus tugs on Gracie's leash and ambles toward the path edging the flood channel. Years before, the Army Corp of Engineers had built a dam in Homestead Canyon, lined the meager stream bed with cement and enclosed it with chain link fencing. He wished they'd let it be. Sybil, his landlady up at the bungalows, claims she played in the creek when she was a girl. Remembers catching trout. Trout! How wonderful, he thinks, if there was trout.

"Dad?" Mars tramps down the path after Gus, grinning.

The old man mutters to himself, "And now, my day is ruined," as he continues to plod along the chain—link fence.

"I knew I'd find you here. Hey Gracie, you dog."

"What'd you want, Mars?"

"Thought we'd go out to dinner, you know, since it's your birthday."

"I don't like missing *Wheel of Fortune*." Gus stops. "Besides, why do I wanna go out and eat somebody else's food?"

"For the fun of it?"

"Fun is saying, 'Time waits for no man' before some doofus shouts it out on TV. Oh never mind. I got a couple of boxes of mac and cheese. If you wanna eat, let's eat." He yanks on the dog's leash, and Gracie trips on her short feet as they turn back, heading home.

He feels Mars' eyes boring into his back. In the old days Mars was the one who stomped off, and the old man wouldn't see him for days. And for a second, Gus imagines his boy at fourteen, kicked out of school, and packing a grocery bag with jeans and t—shirts. Gus had let him go then. He'd let him go now, but when he reaches the street, there's Mars trudging up the path after him.

Inside the bungalow, Gus fills a saucepan with water and puts it on the stove to boil. Mars opens the fridge and brings out a bottle of wine. He grabs two mismatched glasses from the cupboard, one with a stem, one without, pours the Sauvignon blanc, and hands the stemless one to Gus who feels the familiar irritation he always feels when his son is around for more than ten minutes.

"I got a job," says Mars.

"What kind of job?" Good, thinks Gus. Don't want you moving back here.

"You know Ian, that guy next door?"

"The shiny penny? You're gonna work for him?"

"His mother. She has people working for her, you know, when she's got a house to sell. She wants me to run one of her crews, cleaning up yards, painting, moving furniture. They clean 'em up now. Stage 'em, she says."

"Well, don't go walking off with anything. One stint in jail is enough. Thank heaven your mother never lived to see that."

Mars stares at him, clinching his teeth, his body stiff and awkward, just like when he was a boy. "Why do you think I'll never change?"

Gus knows his son is trying, but change is impossible. No, that's not right. Change is unlikely. Whatever Gus's own faults were when he was young, they've magnified with age – impatience, severity, and intolerance. Yes, that too – but he's too old and too tired to make himself change. Mars won't be any different.

Mars says, "You want me to go? I'll go."

"No I don't want you to go." Gus' arm comes up fast to wave off the idea, and Mars flinches. That flinch. The surge of annoyance shooting through Gus requires all his willpower not to turn wave into blow. Mars the man stands his ground where Mars the boy would have thrown himself to the ground. The old man shakes himself, turns quickly to the pan on the stove, lifts the lid and breathes in steam. It takes him a couple moments, frowning at the few tiny bubbles forming around the sides, to regain control. If he'd only said yes to Mars' dinner invitation to go out to eat, they would've been polite. They've always been okay in public, and maybe they'd already be seated at some Mexican restaurant, the waitress scribbling down their order.

The food would come out pronto and they'd eat, both of them keeping their mouths full, and they'd be paying the bill in a half hour or so. Mars would drop him back home and Gus would tell him "don't bother coming in" and off the kid would go. But none of that is possible now. He should've known.

Mars moves around the kitchen, finally settling against the counter, drinking his wine, blocking the two packages of Mac and Cheese. He clears his throat, says, "Did Sybil ever hear from that woman with the two kids?"

"Not that she's ever said." He nudges Mars aside to get to the boxes. Rips off their cardboard tops.

"Where'd she take off to?"

"I don't know. Back to her mother, I guess."

"I think Sybil said she didn't have a mother."

"Then why're you asking me?"

"I'm just making conversation."

Gus lifts the lid of the water again, but it's still not boiling. Spots his own glass of wine, takes a long deep drink, thinks happy damn birthday to me.

There's an awkward silence, then Mars asks, "Her husband ever show up?"

"What're all these questions? You got a thing for her?"

"No. No. Just curious. Seems like she had a tough go of it is all."

"He showed up, asked where his wife was, and when nobody knew, he left to look for her."

"Okay, sorry. I just thought it was strange the way she took off without saying good-bye to anyone."

Gus checks the water. Almost there. Good enough. He dumps in both packs of noodles and stirs it.

"So Dad," says Mars, his voice a little sly. "What'll you do when Sybil sells the bungalows?"

"She'll never sell."

"Mrs. Shane is pretty certain she will. She says she'll help you find a better place, same rent."

"I don't wanna move." Gus glances at the clock over the stove. Too early for *Wheel*.

"But what if you have to?"

"What are you getting at, Mars?"

Mars holds up his hands, palms out. "Just saying, Dad, that Mrs. Shane doesn't want anyone to feel displaced."

"Displaced?"

"That's what she said. She wants to be fair. Which is why I'm giving you a heads up. Since she's my boss, you have an in: *me*. My birthday present to you."

"You're my 'in'? For what?"

"Whatever you want. A new place, a better place. Maybe closer to downtown."

"What about the other tenants?"

"She's happy to help them too. She wants everything to go smooth as silk."

Gus gives his son a hard look, turns away, back to the water and the macaroni boiling over and hissing on the stove. "I bet she does."

Schöne Grüße aus Tirol

by Sally–Anne Macomber

To: Milton Flaxmill, Red Cow Publishing
From: Trudy Polaris
Date: March 20, 2014 10:03 a.m.
Re: Nuclear Fission in the Pyrénées

Liebe Milton,

Greetings from Tirol (or Tyrol)!

How's the editing proceeding with *Nuclear Fission in the Pyrénées*? I'm glad it has such a methodical and tireless editor working on it. I raise *ein Stein Bier* to you!

BTW I was thinking, maybe you might want some assistance, just to speed the editing up a little, because it's taking a little longer than it would normally, probably because summer has hit you early and that red pen can get a little slippy and slidey all over the page.

Once the cows are milked here in our Tyrolean hideaway each morning and I slap them on the rump and put them back in their stalls, I spend the rest of the day twiddling my thumbs, really, and I'd just as soon spend it on something intellectual and hands–on.

I wouldn't even charge you the regular fee.

The spring flowers will soon be here and it's a magical time, so the cowherds tell me in their fractured English. And the fresh mountain air will put hair on your chest too, as a Tyrolean saying goes.

And there's a synergy here with the *cows* outside and you working for Red *Cow* Publishing.

The maître—d' at the Gasthof Traube in Hopfgarten im Brixental asked after you just last night and is looking forward to showing you the town. (He mentioned you'd met once at a Rotary convention in New Guadalcanal.) A local tourist guide says the Traube's a great place 'where you can try meals such as schnitzel, strudel or noodles'. And the town 'also has a renowned church with a wonderful ceiling'. So there's a lot to do here when you down your red editing pen.

The nearest airport is Langkampfen Airport in Kufstein, which is only 30 minutes drive away but there are quite a few heliports which are a bit closer. So there are loads of ways you can get here. Maybe even the local bus would drop you off.

Just let me know the best address to send your ticket to. Or would it be better to download one and email it? Whatever's easiest.

Looking forward to seeing you and getting down to work on the book. I always enjoy being part of a team!

Auf Wiedersehen!

Trudy

Friday, 21ˢᵗ March 2014

Candles

by Mandy Nicol

I'm trying on dresses, deciding what to wear to Tom and Ellie's wedding tomorrow.

I get a lot of wedding invitations. Months of intimate contact seem to compel a bride to invite the lonely little dressmaker.

Usually I decline.

I wish I had declined this one.

Mum told me I'd be mad to go so of course I sent an acceptance straight away. She thought I was mad to make Ellie's dress, too.

Mum thinks I still hold a candle for Tom.

Tom would have thought he was doing a good thing, suggesting Ellie get me to make her dress. Good for my business, he'd have thought, without considering the awkwardness. We had both wanted to stay mates, hadn't we?

I had expected to get at least one chance to stab Ellie with a dressmaking pin. Turned out she's a sweet, uncomplicated girl who I can't help but like. I can see how she turned footloose Tom into marriageable Tom.

I take off my green dress, the emerald green that mirrors my eyes, according to Tom. I'll wear the boring beige instead.

Saturday, 22nd March 2014

Dreaming

by Margaret Bingel

Ned is dreaming about the dogs again. Purple and floppy−eared beagles bounding through fields of pure plaid, with a pale clock bleeding from the sky, melting with the solid blocks of ice Ned thinks are clouds. He watches the dogs while they yip and yelp, sniffing each others' asses and then, recognizing their smell, as they sit on the grass, or at least what Ned is pretty sure is grass.

Ned doesn't know he's been dreaming any of this. For the past two months, he thinks he has been awake. Everything makes sense to him in this place: animals outside, the sun in the sky, even himself barefoot. Ned is at peace, and in no rush to leave.

I love it here, he thinks. Why would I ever leave?

The ice shatters with every hour of the sun−clock, always cracking but never hailing down and hurting Ned or the dogs. But it isn't the threat of death or lack of pain that puts Ned's mind at ease: the hands on the clock don't move. Time Stands Still.

Ned sits down, running his hand over the tartan grass. The fact it is plaid does not bother him, mostly because he's tired from wearing tight shoes all day and needs to take a load off his feet. Breathing in the smell of rosemary and forget−me−nots, he focuses on the dogs.

As he watches the beagles, now panting on their purple backs, their bright yellow eyes drooping in their faces just like the sun dripping in the sky, their chests rise and fall so slowly, like they are as unperturbed by the lack of time as he is. Maybe I should be like that too, Ned thinks, opening his tuxedo jacket and loosening his bow–tie. Maybe I should be more like a dog.

Maybe I should get a dog instead of a gun.

Ned's hand grabs a clump of grass. Why do I want a gun? When did I get a gun?

I never got a gun, he remembers. I never made it to the store.

Suddenly, the clock hands move, at first like paddling through pudding, then faster, like snakes in sand rippling the sky. Faster and faster the clock moves time forward and all of Ned's memories return to him. Ned remembers walking out the door, and seeing two beautiful women, then tripping over ice and then . . .

Ned tries to remember what happens next, but all he sees is emptiness. He focuses on the beagles and they are breathing faster now, in quick gasps, and their colors change to a royal purple, then ashes–of–rose, then anemic pink. Their eyes, now closed, move rapidly under their eyelids, until one of them, the fatter of the two, opens its eyes and looks Ned right in his.

I fell down and hit my head, remembers Ned.

Nora grabs her son's hand and says, "Bye, Boy." She feels a squeeze back. She grabs his other hand and, feeling her son's grip, "Ned," she whispers, her voice choking with tears. She shakes her head.

"Boy, wake up."

Ned opens his eyes and, unfocused, stares at the hospital ceiling.

Sunday, 23rd March 2014

Big Words

by Darryl Price

This day does not deserve its own paragraph.

So I wonder what makes a tree such a good companion when you're out walking alone in the universe?

At least clouds keep their distance.

I wish I could shrink myself down to the size of a blade of grass.

Then nobody could find me.

No one is looking for me that I know of.

But inside the tall blades I'd be like buried alive.

Her enormous green eyes were hazel just like some kind of spin art.

I hate green sometimes, well right now I do I think.

But not really.

What's the point of hating a color?

Hate is useless.

Pretty useless.

The only useful thing is air.

Air and sunshine make a good combination.

I want to go home.

I have no idea where that is.

Instead of shrinking I've enlarged to the size of a house, I'm towering like a tree myself.

I'm standing on top of the earth.

I'm floating off into outer space.

I am my own rocketship.

The heels of my sneakers are spitting plumes of real fire.

I know there's something I'm not supposed to care about any more, but I can't remember what it is.

It hurts too much.

Oh yeah.

This stupid day.

The wind makes more of a pissed off noise than me.

Cars are big dumb animals chasing each other.

I think I think too much.

Monday, 24th March 2014

Another Man

by Teresa Burns Gunther

A moth, wings wide, rests in the globe of the ceiling light. A quitter. Rachel, on her back in her closet, resolves to clean it. The crisp sleeves of blouses and jackets point down at her from their hangers. Normally cleaning gives her satisfaction, but today she's stalled out. Her father is coming.

March is the month she'd set aside on New Year's Eve to purge her house and life of the old and unwanted. It's already March 24th, only seven days left. Her father, Peter Stoddart, theater director – or *theatre* as he insists on misspelling – is a tall, heavy man, handsome in a square–jawed and exuberant way. Life on his planet is an endless E–ticket ride and Rachel knows he sees her as the sorry slob who opted to do the sweeping up.

"The IRS?" he'd asked, incredulous when she'd finished her joint law degree and masters in taxation. "You have gifts. You could have been a concert pianist."

She drums her fingers into the floor regretting taking the day off. It's a busy time at work at the IRS – April 15th is 22 days away. Her phone buzzes with a calendar alert: *Dad. 30 minutes.*

She scrambles up, alarmed. How could it be 11:00? She is not a woman who loses track of time or leaves things unfinished. She is never late. Hurrying to the shower, Rachel nearly trips over Stella, who is used to Rachel's bursts of business and lays on the floor, her lovely head on her paws.

During college, her father questioned her about her degree in math, claiming it boring work for narrow minds. "I like numbers," she'd explained. Numbers are constant, no drama, they embody fidelity. She wonders if there could be another father–daughter combo as mismatched as hers. She's always imagined she'd marry a man who might meet her father head on, bowl him over. But life so far has diverged from her plans for finding a suitable man.

Her father phoned the week before to say he was flying into "Frisco" on the 24th and wanted to see her. She kicks herself for failing to deflect him; she's usually good at putting people off, without even trying. She quickly dries her hair then brushes her teeth, steps 4 and 5 in her morning 10–step–rise–and–shine routine. Her phone buzzes again. *Dad. 15 minutes.*

She settles on a pair of pressed jeans, a turtleneck and scarf that aren't trying too hard, simply making an effort. After slipping into boots she dashes through her apartment, lining up couch cushions, picking a twist of lint off the floor. The large old–fashioned school clock on the wall ticks the remaining 240 seconds, 239, 238 ... She turns the radio to the A's pregame show; the standings and stats fill the room, relaxing her.

He's late. Six minutes. She sits on her leather sofa and stares out at the fog–shrouded skyline. Eleven minutes. Stella curls on her bed watching. "He's coming," Rachel tells her. "And you have my permission to bite."

When her doorbell buzzes she jumps. Stella leaps from her bed, barking as she races to the door. "Good girl!" Rachel smooths Stella's fur standing stiff along her spine. Through the fisheye Rachel is surprised to see an old man, bald. It takes her a moment to recognize her father. She grips Stella's collar and opens the door.

"Rachel!" His arms open wide. Stella growls. He steps back. "Jesus. It that a wolf?"

"Yes," she tells her father though Stella's really a mix of Alsatian, Shepherd and Ridgeback. "This is my father, Stella. I guess he doesn't approve of you, either."

His jeans need pressing; his leather jacket is as worn as his face.

"Do you want to come in?"

"Do you think it's safe?" he asks in his stage voice.

Rachel opens the door wide and orders Stella to bed. Her father stands in the hall, his suitcase beside him. The light from the window is not kind to him.

"You don't look so good," she tells him. "What happened to your hair?"

"Okay." His smile wavers. "Thanks for that." His eyes survey her spotless, symmetrical living room. "Nice place," he says. "How long have you been here?"

"Five years. So nice of you to drop by."

"C'mon, Rach." He drops his chin and gives her an impish smile that works on most women. "Let's have a nice visit." Stella growls and he eyes her warily. "Maybe we could go out for lunch."

"I had a large breakfast," Rachel says, annoyed at her heart's racing betrayal. "Stella and I took a long run."

"Okay. How about a short walk and a quick drink?" He grins, hands in his pockets, like life is easy.

Rachel looks at her watch and raises her brows, though a scotch is tempting. He seems shorter, his middle wider, as if life has pressed down on him, hard. She suggests the coffee house on the corner.

As they walk Peter fills the air with his hands and his chatter about his new season, offering her tickets, inviting her to New York. He greets the neighbors: the cadaverous marathon man from down the street, and the Aussies next door who look surprised that Rachel is related to such a friendly, exuberant man.

§

The windows of Kaffeine's are steamy from the crowd and hot coffee. Her father rubs his hands together and asks, "So, are the numbers behaving at the IRS?"

"What do you want?" she asks, a mug of black coffee cupped in her hands.

He stirs cream then one, two, three large teaspoons of sugar into his coffee.

She looks pointedly at the belly bulge above his belt. "That explains a lot."

"Rachel. Could you try, for once, to give me a break?" He shakes his head.

"Okay. What do you want?" Rachel asks again.

"To see you."

"And?"

He sits back in his chair and studies her. "You really look great," he says.

Rachel waits.

"I thought I might stay for a little while, spend some time together. Just us two."

"We two."

He closes his eyes for a moment. "I have a month before the new season gets underway and …"

Is he suggesting he stay with her? Rachel hasn't had a roommate since her first semester in college. Before he gets to his punch line: another new wife, short on cash, she says, "My landlord won't allow it."

He looks confused. "I thought you owned your place."

"I do. I'm the landlord and the CC&Rs clearly state: no multiple tenancies."

"Is that why you don't marry?"

She considers this, hating to be reminded. "Let's say it's not on my bucket list."

"Is that my fault, too?"

She pushes her coffee away; it's lukewarm and she likes it hot. "I do best on my own."

A waiter appears, disrupting the awkward silence. She shivers at his mutilated earlobes stretched wide with a metal wheel. He tops up their cups and deposits a large chocolate croissant before Peter. Rachel cringes; she hates excess. Her mother indulged him everything, doting and adoring, always his riveted audience, something he must have found irresistible, at first. Now her beautiful mother is in a facility, high−quality care for the demented, and still believes Peter is her husband.

"Do you ever see her?"

"Your mother? I try," he says, the corners of his mouth turn down.

"Do you need money, Peter?" He wants to be called Dad, but she told him years before that "Dad" was a nickname reserved for men who parent.

"No! Of course not, I just want to spend time with my little girl."

Her mother withered after he left them. Rachel was six. Her mother never went to college, had never been told she could be someone else, someone great. At least Peter had given Rachel that.

"Aren't you old for a midlife crisis?" she asks. He's 64. His shoulders drop and for once she regrets the zinger. She avoids his eye. She is so much better with numbers.

He turns at the sound of an ambulance, siren screeching, closing in. His eyes follow the blurred red lights across the steamy windows and in that moment his face, naked of manufactured élan, reveals him. He's lonely! She'd never imagined it possible; his life has always been crowded, standing room only.

He takes a bite of his croissant. His hunger is unbearable to watch.

Tuesday, 25th March 2014

Morgana Malone and the Mystery of the Opium Den

by Matt Potter

Mary Agnes flicks crust from the edge of her mouth with her finger and sits back into the armchair. Tucking in her triple chin, she looks at me and says, "Doesn't she, Morgana?"

In the mirror, I see tears welling in Zebadie's eyes.

(Zebadie's ex−co−star Virginella Vox pulled out last week, due to a Botox overdose, so I'm the lone bridesmaid now.)

Zebadie, blonde nest piled on her head, stands in front of the three−way mirror looking at her own reflection. Poured into a sateen wedding gown that's somehow off−the−shoulder *and* plunging to her navel, it also has a giant hood that I think, in its more gymnastic moments, might double as a train.

A tear rolls down Zebadie's cheek. She turns to look at Mary Agnes, her little teeth flashing, and Mary Agnes looks at me so Zebadie looks at me and then looks back at Mary Agnes. I don't know who to look at, so I stare in the mirror, at the widening grey−and−brown strip showing through my dyed−orange hair.

"Like I said," and fingers drumming on the worn velvet armrest Mary Agnes repeats her pronouncement: "You look like a whore."

I catch Zebadie's eyes again in the mirror. Her shoulders sag, and she looks like a helpless bunny − Playboy bunny; rabbit−

caught−in−the−headlights bunny; victim of someone's cruel joke bunny − so I pipe up: "You mean professionally or do you mean personally?"

"All I said is," Zebadie whispers, the fabric flowers she holds in her hand − the *test bouquet* as the bridal shop assistant told us − jiggling as she shakes, "my right side is better so when we're standing at the altar thing I want to have my right side closer to the cameras and the audience."

There's no denying it, with her three and a half boob jobs, Zebadie's right side certainly creates a larger impression.

Mary Agnes raises an eyebrow.

"This is *my* wedding, Mum, may I remind you," Zebadie says.

Mary Agnes pulls herself up in her seat. Her chins wobble in time with the flowers shaking in Zebadie's hands. "I didn't come here to be insulted, Melissa," − Melissa is Zebadie's real name − "especially when I'm doing you a favour." Mary Agnes slumps back into the chair. "I don't care which side anyone sees as long as it's covered up!"

Zebadie throws the test bouquet on the floor at her mother's feet. The flowers lie squashed and faded, but actually, look quasi−tasteful against Mary Agnes's red diamante−studded wedgies with velvet bows across the toes.

"I should have gone bowling instead," Mary Agnes continues, now waving her flabby arms and jabbing the air with her index finger, like a rapper. "It's the inter−zonal finals for the late Tuesday afternoon Mini−League. But no, you're getting married − again. So I'm helping you choose a wedding dress − again. Looking at you dressed like a slut − again again again!"

I cross my knees and put a finger on my lips, wetting the tip with my tongue. With wobbling chins and heaving bosoms and snapping nerves I can't help but think of Grigor's new nose job and what if Grigor has the same good side as Zebadie? Will they both want their right side to the camera? How will he kiss the bride? When I married Grigor thirteen years ago we had the ceremony in my mother's garden and he kissed me on the mouth afterwards and no one cared about profiles but if they both have the same best side, what will he do after the 'You may now kiss the bride' speech? Kiss her on the back of her head?

And then − I don't know why I say this, but it just flies out of my mouth: "Define *whore*?"

Like I'm the arbiter of all things whorish.

"If you'd loaned me the money I would have been able to get the left one done at the same time, Mum," Zebadie continues, like I'm not in the room. She's sniffing now, four layers of false eyelashes glistening in the yellow bride−to−be light.

I put my hand over my mouth and swallow a yawn.

"And it would have been a tax deduction so I would have paid you back when I got my tax return!" Zebadie says. "So it would have been a win−win−win situation all round," and she points to her mother and then to herself and then to her own left breast.

Reflected in the mirrors, a door opens and a woman of about thirty − tall, long brown hair slicked down and pulled together at the nape of her neck − steps into the bridal sanctum. "Ho−ow's it going?" she asks as our heads snap to watch her. And before there's time for any reply, she looks snivelling Zebadie up and down and says, "Oo−oh! You look gor−orgeous!" The muscles in her face shift upward and her mouth curves into a smile and her voice bounces around the room, but the way her words stretch out isn't convincing: her eyes are wide but their light is extinct.

"You look tired," I say to her in the reflection. She pulls some of the dress fabric away from Zebadie's thigh and, shoulders slumping as she cranes to look, lets it fall. She must have done this thousands of times, I think, to make it look so … spontaneous.

As she pulls more of the dress fabric away from Zebadie's thigh, like she's prepping Zebadie for a fashion shoot or a cakestand, I see her name badge. *Kylie Jay's World of Dream Weddings*, it says, in sparkly silver, and below that, *Hi, I'm Conradine*. But the sparkly silver is scratched, like it was caught on the bottom of her shoe as she walked across cement.

Conradine folds her arms under her breasts, and looks Zebadie up and down again, this time like she's a mannequin in a ... I don't know, a porn bridal shoot.

Zebadie turns to look in the mirror. She flicks out the bottom − or the crown − of the draping hood, and looks at her own bottom in the reflection.

"It's exci−i−ting, isn't it?" Conradine says, watching Zebadie in the mirror looking at her bottom. And as we watch her, Conradine unfolds her arms, laces her fingers together, locks her elbows, and stretching her palms outward, cracks her knuckles. "Ste−epping off into the re−est of your li−ife."

"Stepping in front of a runaway train!" says Mary Agnes.

"Grigor owns a Porsche, Mum!" Zebadie snaps. Like she's saying, *Grigor's developed the patent for world peace, Mum*. Or, *Grigor really loves me for the person I am inside*.

"Hmmm," says Mary Agnes, and shifts her flobbing arms on the worn velvet. We wait for the rest of her retort, but her lips are pursed.

"So, do you thi−ink you'll take it?" Conradine pipes up. "Because it looks one hu−undred percent stu−unning on you, you have ju−u−ust the fi−igure for it."

I watch Conradine's jaw extend and snap to get around those vowels. Maybe talking like that stops her from growing completely bored.

Zebadie shakes her head, and looks downcast at the hem gracing the floor. "I was really looking for something more 50's," she sniffs, the fussy customer again. "A bit more velour. A bit more glam. A bit more shinier. And I don't like the hood."

"We can always take the hood off," says Conradine.

"No, I want it bigger," Zebadie says.

"Were hoods that big in the 50's?" I ask. (I don't know why I do this, the conversation draws me in and words fly out of my mouth.) Now all eyes are on me. "I mean, big as in popular."

"Oh ye—es," says Conradine. "It was the e—e—era of the hood. The hood was derigeu—eu—eur in the 50's. It was only later that pe—eople stopped wea—earing them. When I think hoo—oods I always think 50's. Hoo—oods. Fi—if—ties. Fi—if—ties. Hoo—oods. Hoo—oods. Fi—if—ties. Fi—if—ties. Hoo—oods."

I take it back. I don't think she's staving off boredom with her elongated vowels and snapping jaw. I think she's on laudunum.

The sun blazes deep in the western sky and we're standing by the kerb waiting for Grigor to screech up in his Porsche and drive us all to dinner at a new seafood restaurant right on the wharf at Port Adelaide called *Scabs*. ("I've cancelled all my patients," he told us, as he helped us into a taxi earlier this afternoon. "I can't solve people's deep psychological problems *and* escort them to and from the reception desk at the same time.")

Conradine stands around the corner, foot flat against the brick wall behind her, smoking a cigarette. Her shoulders are relaxed and her eyes are steady. Maybe it's just serving customers inside *Kylie Jay's World of Dream Weddings* that makes her sound like she works inside a centrifuge.

I turn to look at the rush hour traffic. I don't know how we'll all fit in Grigor's Porsche. I remember from the time I mistakenly fucked Grigor inside it, there's not a lot of room in the back seat of a Porsche. The jaws of life would have a hard time extracting anyone from that thing.

Though if Grigor skids into the *Scabs* car park and the Porsche spins off the wharf and we all crash into the water, I plan to grab on to Zebadie's right airbag and not let go. That should keep me afloat 'til the Water Rescue Squad arrives.

Shot

by Gary Percesepe

This happened in Saint Louis. I was a graduate student, and a regular at a half dozen bars. I managed to fail my language examination in German, then French, a language I had studied since seventh grade. By this time I was meeting students after class in bars. The students were female, Catholic, and underage. I made $550 a month as a Teaching Assistant. Rent was $225. Jobs in my field were non—existent. What I did next is that I fucked one of my students, then fucked another.

The first girl was named Ann and the second one I don't remember.

Ann was trying to stop smoking. She sang along to the radio in my rusted Triumph Spitfire. It was winter and I had the top up and the heater blasting. She wore a tartan skirt with a kilt pin and red knee socks. The skirt rode high up her waist and she twitched and sang off key. She was drunk and I was well on the way. Her hair was dark and shiny and she wore one pink barrette, which kept slipping out of her hair.

In class, she tracked my movements. She sat in the second row, just to my right. I smoked in class, which was illegal even for the Jesuits, and came to class half lit after three beers and whiskey shots at Humphrey's bar. Ann liked that I smoked, and teased me about the way I held a cigarette like a joint. Word was out among the undergraduates about my teaching. Student evaluations were among the best in the department, and my classes always closed early. Ann told her parents that she was staying overnight with a friend in West County. From the SLU Library, she called a friend in Ballwin to make sure she had cover. Then she took my hand and walked me out of the library and into my car. She was nineteen with good ID. She set the radio to a station I never used.

We made our way to Rollo, Missouri, where we hooked up with a few of her friends who attended engineering school. Ann made me stop at a grocery store in town where she bought a toothbrush and toothpaste. She told me she hated brushing her teeth with her fingers after a night out. She pulled me into a long sloppy kiss when we stalled in the checkout line. Her small breasts pressed against my chest. She jammed her hand into the back pockets of my Levis and held on.

We got back in the Triumph and drove to a dive bar. Kicking aside some empty longnecks, I jumped the accelerator. Ann lit another cigarette.

Tom Petty and the Heartbreakers wailed *American Girl*. Her friends looked at me, hard. Ann said, "He's a great teacher." I wanted to smile. She looked over and said, "You're a bad guy, you know that?"

We ended up at some guy's house. There was a single bed and we fell into it. I pawed at her. She pushed my hands away and said, "Mmmm, later, I'm sleepy." Ann was too drunk to fuck, so I watched her sleep for two hours. Her small chest rose and fell.

I lit a cigarette and checked my watch. The watch was a high school graduation present, with hands that glowed in the dark. Ann's eyes were shuttered black buttons. She hadn't removed her makeup or brushed her teeth. I parted her lips with my finger and ran it along her teeth until she sucked it. She moaned and turned over. Her pale arms sprawled behind her like a baby seal. Her body took little space on the bed. I felt like a giant. The kilt pin was still fastened to her pretty skirt. I peeled off her knee socks, one at a time and placed them carefully on the hardwood floor. The bed had a small patchwork quilt. I pulled the quilt up over her hips.

After the second hour I pulled the quilt off. I pushed her skirt aside and looked at her plump white thigh. She was small but finely calibrated in that way petite women have, that can drive you crazy if you let it; everything made to scale but fully operational. Her thighs narrowed into runner's calves. I kissed the back of her knees, traced her tendons with my tongue and got as far as her feet, which had red lint between the warm toes.

Ann got up to pee. I watched her go and then she was back. She criss-crossed her arms to remove her sweater. Off came the black bra. The palest nipples, I could barely see them. Her doll's eyes were sightless. I liked how the black bra looked against her white skin, but then the bra was off and tossed to the floor with the socks. She left the skirt on, but reached down with two fingers and twisted her panties aside. "Have at it," she said.

The next night I was at Tom's Bar & Grill. Stephanie wasn't a student. She explained that she was an event coordinator. I bought cocaine from a guy I knew at the bar and told Stephanie. Her sweater smelled of cigarette smoke and White Shoulders perfume. She was working this event, she said, but we'd get together later. I nodded. Stephanie was five ten in strappy heels with long straight hair, a blonde, and her voice was whiskey and soda. Some guy saw the way she looked at me and said, "Sure, her shit don't stink." I turned away toward the wall. Where I watched her in the big mirror Tom had mounted above the bar. The liquor bottles stood like soldiers. Stephanie caught me looking and smiled. Her teeth were white and even and she was tan under all that blonde. She was pretty and slightly used, and I mouthed at her into the mirror, "Sure, I'll see you later."

But I did the rest of my drugs and then poppers and my nerves were jangling and time sped and then slowed, and I nursed a pint and grew tired of waiting for her. Just before leaving I saw her come out of the bathroom, her heels off and slung over her shoulder. She still had a full eight inches over Ann. I told her I couldn't wait for her anymore. She said, "You seem angry," and I said, "No, not angry, just tired of waiting." I left her there and went out to my car.

I went back a week later, and the week after that, and she wasn't there. I asked Tom whatever happened to Stephanie? The leggy blonde with the voice? Tom looked at me (I was a regular) and said, "Stephanie? I don't know any Stephanie, sorry."

Ann struggled to write an analytic paper on Descartes' *Meditations on First Philosophy*. She couldn't understand the Pakistani guy in the writing help room, so she climbed three flights to my dingy office. I sat with her under blinking fluorescent lights, diagramming sentences. Multiple choice threw her, too. Ditto Venn diagrams and Aristotelian logic. We took a cigarette break and walked into the weak Saint Louis sunlight down by the river. She told me she had had twelve years of Catholic school and attended mass until she was sixteen. Then one Sunday, standing in line for communion, she saw a girl her age wearing a T-shirt that said "I love my pussy." Then that was that.

Oh, I liked her.

These were years I counted as lost. Soon I would be married, though I couldn't have known it at the time. Waking up, married, I would think I heard someone crying, then rush through the house, remembering. Outside, bright moonlight on concrete.

I held on and finished my dissertation but there were still no jobs in my field. The teaching continued for a while. I gave up trying to find Stephanie. It was as if she never existed.

There were other students, none I liked as well as Ann. But she was right, I was a bad guy.

The day Reagan got shot I was at Tom's, drinking. The bar exploded in applause. Dan Rather was on the CBS news, remembering dead presidents. Dealy Plaza. This was a bar where guys handed over their paychecks, fifty cent beers the norm. The TAs would huddle together and try not to make eye contact with the regulars. When Dan Rather announced that the president was going to be OK, the bar groaned. One guy threw beer at the TV. A fight broke out. I left the bar and called Ann at her parent's house in Ballwin, but she wasn't home.

Someone once told me, or maybe it was a poet, that marrying is like throwing a baby up in the air, the baby happy and gurgling, and then throwing it higher till it hits the ceiling, jarring the bulb loose, and it goes out as the baby starts down.

I tried to find Ann on the Internet, which led me to idiotic sites like "My Life," which is a joke in itself, right? All I could come up with was her name, her age, and her city. She hadn't moved. I could have paid money to discover more. She'd be twice as old as the girls I see now, in bars, and yeah, in class. More than twice as old.

It'd been late March, all those years ago, when I made that trip to Rollo with Ann in my Triumph. Now it's March again, the month I managed to finish my dissertation, the year after I had Ann in class. I received my doctoral hood the following May. I saw Ann walking to class one day, before I left St. Louis for good, and nodded to her, but she didn't know me, or pretended not to. I taught Maimonides in those days, *The Consolation of Philosophy*, but there didn't seem to be any. Women were my consolation, but even then, every day that passed seemed an assault on a flimsy castle.

There is a time after what comes after one is young, and this is that time. There is a time after that, and I'm headed to it, unsteadily. You tell yourself it will get better, and that joy is aligning yourself with what is most real, and the moments of self−soothing arrive when you say don't cry, I'll get you something better. And you hope for whatever hope is for.

113

I gave Ann a "B" in my course and that's a pity, really, because she tried so hard.

Samford gets a rectal exam

by Nathaniel Tower

Samford is waiting in the office of the proctologist. He is nervous, not because he doesn't want to be anally probed (he doesn't want it, but that's not why he's nervous), but because he's worried that this proctologist is some sort of government spy. He is fairly certain that everyone is a government spy.

Samford has been fornicating with his clone—friend Sarah almost every day for a month. After the first shag, she didn't return for a few days, but she eventually had to get her purse back. Samford never bothered asking about the brochure. He put it in the nightstand underneath the condoms, which he doesn't need to use because she apparently can't be impregnated. Sarah is one of the non—fertile clones, a sort of test specimen. There are several government agencies searching for her, but somehow they can't find her even though she does absolutely nothing to hide herself. Samford is afraid that his apartment is bugged, that one day several government agents will storm inside his house and arrest him for harboring a terrorist clone. They'll throw him in jail forever and perform evil tests on him. In spite of these fears, he still lets Sarah screw his brains out every night. Her moans are the only thing that comforts him, the only thing that makes him feel like a real human. He knows the irony of it all.

Samford thinks of all this as he flips through a copy of *People*. The issue mentions nothing of the clones. Sarah has told him that at least one–quarter of the population now consists of clones, just like her. Well, better than her, she says. Not likely, thinks Samford. He knows without doubt that he is in love with her. Every piece of her is perfect, including her scrumptious ass, which now has far less jiggle in it thanks to the hours and hours of sex. He is glad she is incapable of procreating and that he never has to worry about the menstruation that plagues so many couples. Sarah never has mood swings, and she's always ready to fuck.

Samford is flipping a page in *People* when a nurse calls his name. They are ready to see him. He stands and tosses the *People* on the chair. The nurse gives him a *you–fucking–slob– now–I–have–to–pick–that–up* glance. Samford ignores her annoyance and starts thinking about the pain in the ass he is about to get. It's the first time he's thought about it. He's had this date, March 27th, circled on his calendar for over two weeks, and he's just now realizing what exactly is about to happen. It shouldn't be too bad, since Sarah spreads his cheeks open and shines her phone into his hole every night. "I just can't get a good enough look," she always says.

Samford is taken to Room 3C. He doesn't know why it is labeled as such. He sees no 2C and no 3B. There is no reason to have a 3C. The room is far too cold and his skin looks speckled in the unnatural light. He doesn't criticize the light for being unnatural. He may be unnatural himself. He's hoping the proctologist can shed some light on this.

A nurse comes in and takes his blood pressure. 120 over 70. "Is that normal for you?" she asks. Samford says he thinks so, although he isn't sure when his blood pressure was last checked.

"You must have a very healthy lifestyle," she says before leaving.

He doesn't stop her to tell her that all he does is sit around his house, eating chili mac and reading about government clone conspiracies while waiting for Sarah to come home and fuck him. He has no idea what Sarah does all day, but he is sure it is much more productive than what he does. Maybe she even does something that pays the bills. It doesn't really matter to him. As long as each day ends with sex. Although he often worries that he might be a clone, sometimes he is convinced that he must not be because of how horny he is. Even with the nightly fornications, sometimes amounting up to four or five orgasms, he still finds himself jerking off three or four times a day, often to the website www.clonedbitches.com, which is the only porn site he has ever subscribed to. The bitches are furious with their sex, but he doesn't find them as sexy as Sarah. If she ever agreed to do a video with him, he'd stop watching these crappy videos. At least that's what he tells himself.

Samford also finds at least five hours a day for couch napping, often with videos from the Cloned Bitches website streaming on his TV. Sometimes, he wakes up and wonders who pays for his internet. He hasn't paid for anything for as long as he can remember.

The door smacks open against the wall and the doctor barges in. Samford wonders why he doesn't knock first. Then he realizes it doesn't matter. This man is about to be in his ass anyway.

"So how can I help you today?" the doctor says. Samford wonders if the doctor just sticks his finger up butts all day. Surely he must do something else during the eight hours he spends at the office, minus the hour for lunch and the other hours when he sits in his office doing nothing.

"I need a rectal exam."

"Of course you do. That's all you people ever want."

Samford wonders if the doctor is trying to be funny. Maybe this is an icebreaker, a way of getting to know each other before the intimate deed.

"Can we just get this over with?" Samford asks.

"Fine. Drop your pants and bend over on the table."

Samford has seen many Cloned Bitches in this same position. He knows just what to do. He thinks about propping up a leg to give the doctor deeper penetration.

Samford hears the glove snap and the squirt from the bottle of lubricant. He wonders if it's the same type Sarah sometimes rubs on his dick when she wants him to stick it in her ass. He also wonders if she ever poops and how all the wiping would affect the serial number.

"You may feel some slight discomfort," the doctor says, but the finger is in Samford's butt before he can even prepare for the discomfort. It actually isn't uncomfortable at all. It only lasts a few seconds before the finger is out and the glove snaps off.

"Looks fine," the doctor says. "You can pull up now."

"That's it? Don't you want to look up there?"

"Are you fucking serious? What are you, one of those fetish weirdos?"

Samford turns around, but he doesn't pull his pants up. His cock and balls are just hanging there, shriveling up in the cold while he tries to muster the strength to make them look not embarrassing.

"Doc, I need you to look. I think there might be something in there?"

"Don't tell me you are one of those homosexuals who shoves things up your butt. I had these two queers who came in once and –"

"I'm not gay," Samford says. He finds the doctor's speech mildly offensive, but he doesn't blame the doctor. He understands that someone who shoves his hand up butts all day has to do something to reaffirm his love for vaginas.

The doctor frowns, like he's apologizing for his comments. "I didn't mean anything by it. Gay guys are okay."

"Can you please just look? I just want to know if there's anything in there."

Samford thinks about winking, to give the doctor a hint about the serial number. Surely a doctor who touches butts all day knows about this. Samford can't be the only one.

"Okay, I'll have a look. Get back into position."

The doctor opens a drawer and Samford hears him fumble with some tools. Then the snapping glove. Then the squirting lubricant. The doctor doesn't mention the discomfort he may feel this time. As the cold metal shaft slides up his butt and spreads him open, Samford can think only of Sarah and how she has taken a liking to playing with his butthole for a few minutes at the end of each round of sex. A flicker of an erection comes and goes, and then the tool is removed and Samford's butt is back to normal. The glove snaps off.

"Well?" Samford asks as he turns his head, still leaning over the table.

The doctor shakes his head hard. "I didn't see anything. Nothing at all." Then he rushes out of the room without giving Samford a chance to ask anything. Samford's heart starts racing. He knows something is up. The doctor must've seen a serial number up there and is off to report him. He pulls on his pants and bolts out of 3C. He hurries past the receptionist's desk and rushes through the waiting room. On his way out of the building, he starts calling Sarah to tell her what he's done. Then he decides to hang up. He doesn't want to risk losing out on sex tonight.

Friday, 28th March 2014

Reunion

by Kimberlee Smith

My husband Dean hasn't seen me in months, but I get a feeling he will today. Ever since the snakebite, I've developed a constant but slowly intensifying extra sensitivity, a perception as to what might occur in the world. This is something new to me, just since I've been gone. When I mean gone, I mean dead.

Dean's headed out today on a trip with his business partner, Junior Volpe, in that little rusted–out tin can Junior owns and pilots. It's a single–prop Cessna that's older than he is – and that's over half a century of hard living. Junior flies the two of them around the country to "attend to their transactions," as Dean says, in an attempt to sound professionally legitimate in a business that's anything but. What they do is buy and sell deadly snakes on the black market. What they do is illegal. Here in Australia where only native species are legally allowed to exist, it's against the law to keep them as pets.

That goes back to a hard lesson learned when cane toads were imported from Hawaii in the 1930s to deal with the cane beetle bugs eating up all the sugar cane crops. As luck and the Darwinian theory of evolution would have it, the cane toad thrived. And so did the cane beetle. So importing any new species of reptile into Australia was outlawed. There's that little bit of history for you. I learned it all from Dean.

Even though he didn't finish school, he only went up until Year 11, he knows a lot. He has that raw smartness that even some people who go through years of university do not.

What Dean and Junior specialize in are deadly and beautiful snakes. Colorful or killers. What I particularly don't approve of is their brokering endangered species. I observed a little while ago one of their smugglers bringing a stunning and supremely rare San Francisco garter snake back from the United States. The snake's brilliant coloration and striped pattern make it look like a psychedelic rainbow.

The courier had that poor snake sewn up in between two pieces of leather like it was in a sleeping bag and he wore it as a belt to get it from Los Angeles to Sydney. He traveled about eighteen hours with a live animal strung through his belt loops. That particular breed is on the U.S. endangered species list, which makes owning one so desirable, which also means it costs a lot of money. Something like $30,000. That particular type of snake isn't venomous; can't do a thing to you but give you a set of silly little puncture wounds. So it's the perfect creature for a coward to show off.

Dean and Junior have a handful of runners like the guy I just told you about who I never met but I get to know them now like I'm looking through a one−way mirror. Dean and Junior handle all the business within Australia on their own; their employees take the riskier, long−haul international trips.

I know it seems odd there's a thriving underground business in buying and selling exotic snakes, especially in a country known for an abundance of dangerous species, but sure as I'm *here* and you're *there*, it's a fact. Take my word for it, because I've experienced it firsthand. It provided us with a really nice lifestyle. But boy did we pay a price for that.

§

I never met Dean's clients in my life. But ever since that coral snake made a picnic out of my leg and injected enough venom with its fixed fangs to stop my heart for good, I've been privy to much more about who he deals with than I got to know when I was alive. I don't harbor any ill will against the snake, it wasn't doing anything but what nature told it to do. But Dean could have been more careful in keeping them.

With regard to the business end and the people he dealt with, I know Dean was trying to protect me, because the less you know about that kind of business, the better off you are. Now I see who he meets up with, and it's a good thing he never brought them around our home or family. All kinds of shady folks.

There's a man with a skinny little moustache and a jumble of tattoos spreading all down his arms and back, mostly of naked ladies and skulls. He never, ever wears a shirt, but always has on his trucker hat with a cartoon of a bulldog smoking a cigar on it. He's a drug manufacturer, for a living. Cooks up methamphetamine and uses a good amount of it, too. I've watched him smoke it, snort it, and even shoot it between his rotten toes.

Dean has a suspicion but doesn't inquire about the man's business. So now that I can, I followed him back to his house all the way out in Mudgee, and the little building he tells people is a granny flat in the wild bush out back is a filthy drug–cooking factory that looks like it's guaranteed to blow up any second. His littlies are wandering around outside in soiled nappies while their mum screams at them for reasons I can't discern. I wanted to snatch them away, clean them up, tell them they're perfect and not to listen to anyone telling them anything different. It breaks my heart that I saw it all going on and was powerless to do anything about it. Those children are doomed.

Then there's the rotten excuse for a human being who owns a brothel in Parramatta and has his own sisters working as prostitutes. It's not against the law, but that doesn't mean it's right, either. That scum has no qualms with collecting money from his sisters getting banged by married men on their lunch hours, during happy hour, all day and all night long.

The big shot who Dean held onto the pair of coral snakes for has a dominatrix den hidden next to his wine cellar. He keeps the snakes in fancy boxes lining the walls of his pervert palace. He's the man who now owns the snake that bit me. He lives in Rose Bay. Has a mansion on the waterfront with a rock pool and a lovely antique sailboat that once raced in the America's Cup. He's married and his and the wife's children have gone off to university, so now it's just the two of them. His wife travels out of town a lot with her mates for something they call *spa weekends.* They play tennis and get massages and have their nails done. I understand why the wife leaves every so often, given his sexual proclivities that she wants absolutely nothing to do with.

From what I can glean, he brought it up once − waving around a pair of fishnet hose and a ball gag − and that was that. Poor woman fainted cold, hit the floor and got a big old bump on her head. Neither ever brought it up again. The wife's in what you'd say is a classic state of denial. Her absences give him plenty of time to entertain at home. Dean hates that man. He handed off the corals as soon as the man returned from a business trip and never told him what happened to me or with the snakes.

Even though the clients I've found out about come from every conceivable background and lifestyle, what they have in common is the urge to be perceived as badass motherfuckers. They're nothing but weak and insecure. But business is business and Dean has a family to support.

§

A month before baby Etheline was born, Dean spent an afternoon threading together over twenty rattles from snakes he traded, captured, bought, and sold. His is a word–of–mouth business that built steady and fast. Dean has a solid reputation. I'm not saying good, I'm not saying bad. He always delivers the goods he promises his clients.

He wasn't scared of shit until I got bit. And it's not the snakes he's afraid of; it's about his whole world changing in a flash. *His* whole world.

The rattles he fashioned together as the gift for our little girl were from snakes that died in transit or were returned to him because the owners did not have one iota of knowledge how to care for their strange new pets, so the serpents often ended up dying due to overfeeding or lack of or overexposure to heat or light. Dean learned after years of watching his father run a pet shop that specialized in reptiles and birds. He ran the snake business on the side.

People interested in keeping exotic animals are know–it–all tough guys who feel compelled to act as if they know what they're doing and are in control at all times. Dean explains to them like it's a technicality – like he's a carnie regurgitating safety rules for riding a carousel – but he sells fanged, venomous, strangulating snakes with printed out instructions that go something like this: "Feed live rodents but only as directed per your specific breed. Provide fresh, clean water. Keep terrarium locked at all times, except when feeding or cleaning. Maintain a stable temperature consistent with the needs of your particular reptile." Mostly they fuck up.

Dean is unique in his business, like a reputable dog breeder. If something goes wrong, he will take that creature back, dead or alive.

§

I follow Dean mostly. I rarely leave his or our baby's side. When I look down on Etheline, I swear she smiles up at me. I've tried to make contact with Dean, too, but he's been entirely unaware of my presence. Today I'm going to try a little harder.

I'm getting used to my place here in the afterworld. People use the term *afterlife* to describe where I'm at, but let me tell you there's no life here. When it's your time and you arrive, you'll see. It's lonely. There's no one else, just me so far. No angels, no long−lost relatives. I thought maybe I might meet up with my grandmum but no luck yet. I do keep hoping.

I can see Dean, my mum Maybell, and our baby girl who was born right as I died. Baby Etheline was taken from my womb by an emergency C−section. That was the strangest thing, hovering above in spirit watching my own daughter enter the world not five minutes after pronouncing me deceased. Everyone was crying. Even the nurses and the doctors. Terrible tears of pain and some of joy for the baby's survival.

Dean and Maybell take care of the little one, and they do a pretty good job. They trade off, like in shifts. But when one isn't watching the baby, they're drinking hard. Dean likes his beer more than ever; he's up to a six−pack a day when he isn't watching the baby. Maybell splashes gin in her lemon squash. She started that up right after the funeral to numb herself, and she hasn't stopped. Sometimes she puts in more than just a splash. And sometimes she starts at brekkie. They're both just having a hard time coping. I can see that.

§

Dean and Junior are scheduled to make a few different stops on today's trip, which includes a number of stops and is also their biggest day of business ever. They're in Junior's plane, flying out of a mowed down field behind Junior's ranch in Dubbo. They cram four rubber bins filled with snakes into a plane that barely fits two men comfortably. Dean holds an empty metal cash box between his feet. First stop, one bin goes. Cash fills the box. Takeoff. Somewhere outside Adelaide. They've got about half a dozen stops to make at legitimate private airstrips to refuel. Their last stop is outside Perth, and it's windy as hell. They land hard and Dean hits his head, but not bad enough to do anything more than his rubbing it and making some joke. All the snakes are sold, and the moneybox is heavy with bills.

I haven't yet tried to get Dean's attention. I've been waiting for the right moment. But I have been along on the entire journey. Junior all of a sudden pulls a bottle of vodka out from under his seat and takes a long swig. Then he throws that on the floor while the plane is bouncing around in some really wild wind. Dean is drenched in sweat. It's dripping down his temples and his hair is soaked and his shirt is soaked and it's stuck to his chest.

There's a mountain range and a wind farm with about five turbines spinning like crazy a few miles away, but instead of diverting the plane around them, Junior pulls a gun out of his vest and cracks Dean across the face.

Now it's time for me to show up. I take Dean's head in my arms and instead of feeling like a vapor when I've tried to touch him before, he feels solid against me. There's a warm stream of blood dribbling from his ear. His brain is bleeding. He's shaking and the color drains from his face. I put my lips against his cheek and tell him I'm there. His heart races, jolts, and he whispers my name. Over and over. Because I'm finally able to connect with him, neither of us is paying any attention to anything else.

I feel something horrific coming on. Worse than anything before. My energy is on Junior, and he's strapped on a parachute and clutching the moneybox. He hollers in a raspy, evil voice, *fuck you! fuck you!* then punches his window out and dives out of the plane.

Dean is screaming he doesn't know how to fly and I can't do a thing physically to help. But I've been watching Junior fly this thing today and I'm stunned that apparently Dean never paid a lick of attention to how to take over if something were to happen to Junior. He is utterly clueless. Kept his focus on the snake crates, always.

I tell him to hold the yoke with both hands, keep it still and straight. He *can* maneuver the plane around the turbines. I'm doing my damnedest to encourage him, but I am *terrified*. For him, not for me. I tell him to bank around the wind farm, to slowly pull up on the yoke and that will tip the nose down, but he has to do it gradually. The plane will descend steadily under his control. He grips the yoke like he's choking it and his knuckles go white. This mighty windstorm throws the plane every which way, and now it's nose diving. And that's it.

There's an explosion. Fire and metal in a roiling ball of burned flesh and fuel and then nothing identifiable remains. Only smoke, ash, and charred metal.

Off in the distance I see Junior. His parachute knotted up into a blade of the wind turbine's rotor, and he's spinning around, impaled on a blade, like a skewered rag doll. Soon he's shredded into oblivion. Maybell will see it on the news tonight. She will know who it is even before the dead are identified.

The emergency crew can't recover any remains until the gale subsides, because one thing about a turbine is that it stops and goes with the wind. There is no way to control it.

Dean asks me where we are. And all I can communicate is *Together.*

Saturday, 29th March 2014

Winter Weight

by Vanessa Weibler Paris

The Lunch Ladies are crabby today. Even crabbier than usual, since it's the end of the fiscal quarter, which means a mandatory Saturday at work.

The Lunch Ladies are all stabbing their salads. Linda's on her second plastic fork after breaking two tines off the first. Darlene moves her Tupperware a few inches with every forceful pierce. A pink−tinged piece of iceberg, accidentally ejected by someone, plays small sad centerpiece on the round grey laminate.

I'm eating a salad, too. I try to get bites from dish to mouth without them seeing the details: the shreds of cheese, the seeds, the bacon, the beans. The protein. The calories. Anything that might help. My hand, holding the fork, is almost like a flesh−colored fork itself. At my latest doctor's appointment, I got on the scale facing away from the numbers. *Don't tell me,* I wanted to beg the nurse. But I didn't. And she didn't. I heard her inhale sharply after the numbers settled. And then she asked me to please follow her to the exam room.

The Lunch Ladies' meals are watery and insubstantial, pale greens of lettuce and celery and cucumber stuck together with sweet sticky fat−free dressings.

"Celery has negative calories," remarks Barbara, as she does at least once each week. "It takes more energy to chew and digest celery than what's even in it."

It's the same every year. On January 2nd, they all come in with New Year's Resolutions. For a month or so, everything's very cheerful and optimistic and gung–ho. By the end of March, no one's lost much – if any – weight, they're all hungry and tired, and spring break is looming.

I know what comes next: When summer arrives, they've all given up, and resolutions are replaced with the promise of backyard BBQs, burgers and beers.

"We'll start over in the fall," someone will announce, and the rest will agree. And then fall becomes winter, and winter brings holidays, and then it's January 2nd again.

"So does lettuce," adds Dar. "Negative calories. You can practically lose ounces by eating a whole head, if you do it all at once."

At the far table, everyone bursts into laughter, and then a quick hiss hushes them back to whispers. It's the Young Professionals. The ones with bigger cubicles and better titles. The ones with perfect bodies in fitted workwear and shoes that click as they walk. No sad homemade salads for them; it's all takeout. Sushis and schnitzels and souvlakis. Exotic things from fancy food trucks.

At 29, I should be a Young Professional. Instead, I'm the one man among the Lunch Ladies, none under 50. We wear soft–soled comfort shoes that pad slowly through the halls. We all wear oversized clothes – cheap, because we'll save up to buy the real ones soon … once we get to a better size. Once I gain weight, once they lose. Once I look normal. If.

"Don't eat too much," a blonde named Laynie sings out as the Young Professionals stroll by. "Remember there's birthday cake for Brad this afternoon."

We continue crunching until they're gone.

"Goddammit," Linda mutters.

"Goddamn cake," adds Dar, through her teeth.

"Wasn't your birthday last month?" Barbara asks, after a few silent minutes have passed. "Wasn't it, Jim?"

"Not really," I say. "It was the 29th. And there was no 29th."

All my life, I've gotten the question: *Oh, you're a Leap Day baby! How interesting! When do you celebrate? The 28th, or the 1st?*

Whichever is more convenient, I always say, smiling. But that's not true. If it's not a Leap Year, I don't celebrate at all. It doesn't seem right to make myself the center of attention. To make the rest of them look at me, smiling. Pretending to be pleased rather than repulsed.

"We still could've gotten you cake," Linda says, after a pause. She's licking the last bits of sugary dressing from her fork, now down to three tines.

"That's okay," I say. "I don't really like cake anyway."

The Blind Date

by Joanne Jagoda

Anne has the twins drop her off a half hour early for her blind date. She can't stay home another minute. Her stomach has been doing flip−flops all day. Robin is her smartass best on the drive to the restaurant. She shakes her finger at her mother.

"Now Mom, be sure to keep your curfew, no kissing on the first date and call if you're going to be late."

Anne acts like she's annoyed but smiles as she closes the car door. "Very funny. Bye." The twins drove her crazy all day, bubbling over with excitement.

Anne strides in to the grand lobby of the elegant Fairmont Hotel, her head held high, confident she looks good. The lobby is carpeted in a deep burgundy, with mahogany walls, dark green velvet chairs and paisley sofas.

They didn't let up last month until she agreed to try the on−line website they found. Anne looked at different profiles but one stood out, ... *retired patent attorney, likes fine dining in San Francisco, wine tasting in the Napa Valley, hiking and traveling.*

When she got up her courage to respond, 'Eric' emailed her back. She was hesitant at first but gave him her phone number. He was charming when he asked her to dinner.

"Anne, let's try *Jupiter,* in the Fairmont lobby. The chef was just awarded two Michelin stars."

"That sounds perfect, Eric." Anne doesn't know one chef from another because Paul was a meat and potatoes guy, and they mostly went to chains.

She finds a velvet armchair hidden by a lush areca palm where she can discreetly watch the front of the restaurant. Well−dressed couples glide by. Hipsters in sport coats and blue jeans and attractive young women in boots, tights and short skirts sit in the lobby sipping cocktails and checking iPhones. Anne picks at her cuticles. *Why does it look so easy for them? I can't remember what it's like to have fun.*

The girls had given her a gift certificate for a makeover for her birthday. She loved her massage, the haircut and sassy red highlights. A makeup artist made her hazel eyes pop, and with blush and plum lipstick, she walked out a new woman. Robin and Cassie went through her closet tossing the baggy clothes, anything black or gray, which was half her stuff. They took her shopping and helped her pick some snazzy new clothes and selected her outfit for tonight; an elegant fitted black pencil skirt with a pretty off white, lacy blouse, a killer belt and high heeled sandals. Early this morning, she went for a manicure and pedicure, bright red. Anne didn't recognize herself in the hall mirror.

Hiding behind greenery, she is as self−conscious as a thirteen−year old going on her first date. Drips of sweat roll down her back. *Great … I'll have a damp spot on my blouse.* Anne glances at her watch. *He's late. OK … just three minutes.* The three minutes turn to twenty. She checks her cell but no message. After a half hour, Anne curses under her breath. *I can't believe he stood me up. Maybe he was in an accident. I'm getting a drink.*

She waits another fifteen minutes, then heads to the lobby bar, gets up on a leather stool, figures, *what the hell,* and orders a *Cosmo.* She sips the strong drink but when she checks out couples at small tables laughing and talking, a lump in her throat makes it hard to swallow. In all her fantasies about tonight, she never imagined that her date wouldn't show. He was so friendly, asking her questions about her job and the girls.

Damon Southeby, who has been stalking Anne for the last few months, arrived earlier at the Fairmont and sat in the lobby where he could watch for her. He was surprised she looks so hot – compact and sexy, with a trendy cut and a fetching sprinkle of freckles ... much better than she looked two months ago when she was depressed about her fiftieth birthday, as he knew from reading her diary. Damon created 'Eric' for his phony on-line website. Even Eric's voice was distorted with a voice synthesizer. A few keystrokes and Eric Baxter, attorney, existed in the virtual world. A few keystrokes tonight and he'll disappear just as fast.

Ah, so devious, so brilliant. Damon knows he's a cruel bastard but little Anne is part of a much bigger scheme that will net him a huge payday. He watches her expression change from hopeful to glum. Now she's sitting in the bar and he quickly approaches her when an empty seat opens next to her.

"Miss, is this stool taken?"

Anne doesn't answer until she realizes that the gorgeous tall hunk with messy brown hair to his collar, a smile like Robert Redford, and the cutest English accent is speaking to her.

"Uh, no." He takes the empty seat and orders a beer.

"This is a grand hotel," he says turning to her.

"Yes, it is one of the oldest in San Francisco."

"Are you from here?"

Anne can't believe he's talking to her and she blushes because he's checking her out down to her red painted toenails. "No, I was born in Sacramento but I've lived in the Bay Area for years. I take it you're not from here."

"I guess my accent is a giveaway. I'm from a village near London. *David Lewis*. Nice to meet you."

"Hello, I'm uh Anne." She won't tell him her last name no matter how good-looking he is.

"I just moved here four months ago to open the San Francisco branch of my business. We have branches all over the world. Here's my card."

Anne takes his card. *Digital Maneuvers – David Lewis, CEO*, she reads, and places it on the bar.

He grins his best Redford smile. "Miss … uh, is it 'miss?'"

Her smile is strained. "I'm a widow."

"Ah, well I'm so terribly sorry." Damon gives her a sympathetic look. He says in a quiet voice, "I guess we have that in common. I'm a widower myself."

Anne doesn't know what to say. Then David/Damon stands up.

"Uh, Miss Anne, I have a business meeting now and you might find this forward, but perhaps if you would like to show me some of the sights of this fine city you could call me. You have my card."

David gives a little salute and leaves Anne staring. She gets off the stool shaky from the Cosmo, not quite believing what just happened.

She totters through the lobby on her high–heeled sandals, tempted to take them off and walk barefoot. She asks the bellman to get her a cab.

The cab driver checks her out in the back seat. "Where to Miss?"

She laughs, "Just home. Where else would a slightly drunk fifty–year old mother of teenagers go?" She is silent as the cab speeds from Nob Hill to her home in the Sunset district, the skyscrapers of downtown passing in a blur.

When she opens the door she hears the girls upstairs laughing and playing Maroon Five. Anne calls out, "Rob, Cass, I'm home." Slipping off her sandals, Anne looks at her fancy toes. *What a crazy night.*

The girls hear her and come down the stairs. Cassie blurts, "Mom, you're home already? Was he a *dweeb?*"

Anne opens the Frig door and pulls out cold pizza. She shakes her head. "He didn't show. And never called. I assume he didn't call here either."

"Oh Mom," they say in unison, and Cassie goes to hug her.

Anne puts down the pizza and gives Cassie a squeeze.

"What an *asshole*, Mom."

"Robin do you have to use that language?"

"Well he is and I'm pissed. Mom you looked hot tonight. How could he stand you up?"

"It's really OK. Tonight was a dry run. I promise I'm not giving up. But I did meet some cute guy at the bar from London. He gave me his card ... but I'll probably never call him. 'Night kids. I'm getting a headache."

Anne feels badly for the girls who were as excited about tonight as she was. She drags herself upstairs and closes the door to her room. When she takes off her cute new clothes, she lets them fall in a heap on the carpet and puts on her old sweats. She doesn't want to feel sorry for herself. She's done with that.

Across the street sitting in his nondescript Ford, Damon Southeby *or Daniel Lewis* has followed her home. He takes a long sip from a bottle of water watching the lights flicker on in her upstairs bedroom window. He sees her shadow. *There is something sweet and innocent about you Anne Donaldson, and you're very attractive. I'm going to enjoy the perks of this assignment.*

Rinse and Repeat

by h. l. nelson

Dear Diary,

This is how I feel lately:

> *6:02 A.M.: Alarm blares. Abruptly wake. Hit alarm so husband can sleep longer. Stifle urge to hit husband instead. Jump out of bed. Shower. Blow—dry hair. Apply makeup. Put on mom costume. Walk down hall to kids' rooms. Wake them for school. Same thing, Monday through Friday, August through May. Rinse and repeat. This is your life on motherhood.*

Yes, I wrote that. I may have a knack for writing, who knows? What I do know, and hate to admit, is that I never really wanted children. Fuck, I wrote it. I know that sounds terrible. I feel terrible writing it. And this is a really heavy subject for 7:30 on a Monday morning. But, I realized recently it's the truth and I need to admit it to someone or something.

I just want to paint. I'm not one of those women who needs children to fill a void within themselves. The women who, when their kids leave home, wander aimlessly from morning until night, unable to concentrate, work on their hobbies, or keep up with their friendships. While the kids are still at home, they are shells, trying to fill their own voids with ballet, oboe lessons, Kids' Art for Charity events, living vicariously until the day those kids leave. It's sad.

Like all days, this morning I strode into my teens' rooms in turn, exactly 30 minutes after waking, and attempted to gently pat them awake. Dr. Sears suggested this less stressful method. Why I still give a fuck about what Dr. Sears says, I have no idea.

Truth be told, some mornings I feel like slapping the kids awake. Ugh, I'm a terrible mom. But sometimes I despise the little brats. They're typical spoiled, suburban teens who take me and everything they have for granted. Like what happened with Kendra earlier. I suppose it's my own fault. Somewhere deep down, I'm sure I must love being a mom, but I had no idea it would be so hard.

So this morning, Kendra texted me while I was cooking breakfast. The text read: "Cn u gt hollister hoodie frm clset. In shwr." Honestly, I wasn't sure that was even English. Of course, Kendra was in her room when she texted, not the shower. But I still retrieved it for her. It's no wonder they're spoiled. Oh, and I don't even want to write about Kurt. I think he might be doing drugs, but I haven't caught him yet. I ransacked his room and nothing. I still think he's hiding something. Sigh.

You know, I clearly remember being pregnant, like it was yesterday. My ideas about it at first were set by the myth that it's 'a beautiful, life–changing event' and that pregnant women are 'glowing bastions of health'. My pregnancies were indeed life–changing events. I was sick every day. Not just mild nausea, mind you. Daily wracking, heaving vomiting. I lost forty of the fifty pounds I'd gained. Doctor Bailey feared for Kurt's life.

Once we made it through the hellacious pregnancy and Kurt was a newborn, I realized that having a new baby is like giving your number to a drunken stranger in a bar. Both will bug you incessantly at 2 A.M. until you pick up. And will alternate between crying and nursing their drinks all night long. Some say the parent thing gets easier. But as kids age it just gets more complicated. Young girls get periods and cry a lot in the bathroom. Young boys get awkward and also spend a lot of time in the bathroom. Complicated.

As the kids grew up, I vacillated between parenting and self-help books, hoping to get a handle on how the hell to do it better. During upswings, it was the parenting books. Always a new method. Unparenting. You know, the parenting method that suggests it's okay to leave kids in their Superman underwear for days at a time, to let them eat M&M's all day while watching SpongeBob. Unconditional Parenting. This one suggests you shouldn't get angry with your child, that you must remain calm and in control, even if he, demon that he is, is flushing his sister's head in the dirty toilet. Hypnosis Parenting. This one offers no suggestions for situations such as your dog bounding in on one of your hypnosis sessions and your son barking for weeks afterward. It's all bullshit.

On downswings, which happened right after finishing a parenting book, I was on to the self-help ones. *The Secret. Who Moved My Cheese? Awaken the Giant Within.* Books by Dr. Phil. When I read *The Secret*, I meditated for two weeks, envisioned myself as an amazing, loving parent with adoring children and all of the answers. I even wrote out an affirmation and tacked it to my wall. Every morning, I awoke to 'I am the best mom' and started to feel like it was true. Then Kurt told us he had gotten his girlfriend Shelly pregnant and Kendra ran away from home, both in the same week. I was beside myself with guilt and worry. We took care of Kurt's problem, found Kendra and put her in therapy, and I burned that fucking book in the fireplace. Bullshit, bullshit, bullshit.

Sometimes I read romance novels, just for a break. When I was a kid, I swore I would never read those damn things like my stepmom did. I had hated Danielle Steele and loved Stephen King. How things change when we age. We crave sweet, brain-deadening escape.

I've been a SAHM for years, but I dress as if I have a "real" job, as they say. In case anyone reads this and doesn't know, SAHM isn't short for anything kinky. Unfortunately. Stay–At–Home Mom. No wonder someone made it an acronym. It sounds boring. Every time I say it when someone asks what I 'do,' I almost yawn. Even the words "stay–at–home" can't stand alone. They need hyphens between to keep them from falling over in boredom.

"Mom," however, doesn't need any hyphens. It stands alone. Just like I do, since my husband works long lawyer's hours. In this house, "mom" is also synonymous with "slave". I laughed until I cried when I read author Lauren Kessler's blog post: "Being an American mother means you prescribe to this axiom: I am available, at your beck and call, 24/7. Don't even think about what else I might have on my plate or who I am as a person in addition to being your mother. I have no life other than to serve you."

These days I feel less ballsy than my namesake, Joan of Arc. In my younger years, I was more like Joan Jett, going to rock concerts, smoking weed, and sliding myself into leather outfits. The only rock concerts I see now are the ones I drop Kurt off at. Weed, sure – in the backyard. They are always getting into my vegetable garden. Leather outfits – not unless Kendra wants to die young.

Brandon and I haven't done anything kinky with leather in a while. Hell, these days I'm afraid to make a mess on our leather sofa – such a far cry from sex–crazed, twenty–something me. There wasn't an unmessed leather couch in my wake.

I don't think, the way this is going, that I'll put much in this diary like, 'Today, dear diary, I tried a new soufflé and it was just divine. Brandon and the kids delicately ate it all and asked for more. Being the amazing housewife and mother that I am, I had made another and brandished it from the kitchen to a flurry of applause from my loving family.' Fuck. That.

Maybe I'm not cut out for this housewife and mom thing. Maybe I was never meant to have kids. Maybe I should have a large, city studio / apartment with my art up everywhere and a new lover every week. Maybe I should be fucking on large canvasses, covered in paint, with said lovers. Their skin and mine blending colors in never—before—imagined shades, these paintings selling for tens of thousands each. Right. Instead, the food stains on the countertops and on my housewife sweats are blending in never—before—imagined hues, and it's my job to clean it all up. On that happy note, I'm out.

Before I go feel sorry for myself some more, I do have some questions for you. I want to know what happened to my youth? Where did it run off to when I wasn't looking?

And my dreams. I see them so clearly, as if I'm staring at them through bulletproof glass that I will never penetrate. Kurt and Kendra, I love them so much, but, god help me, I always wanted more. And now that I have so much time to myself in the house, I just can't do it. I can't muster the energy and will within myself to pick up a paintbrush, daub on some paint, and go for it. What the fuck is wrong with me? Maybe the moms' group can help. Yeah. I'll call Julie and Robin.

Anne can go fuck herself.

Joan Not—a—Famous—Painter Colderman

Authors

Rachel Ambrose is a twenty–something fiction writer from Connecticut. Her favorite season is winter, she enjoys well–made Manhattans, and she loves Southern fiction. Her work has appeared in *Crack the Spine*, *Exiles Literary Magazine*, and *The Colton Review*. She is currently at work on her second novel and blogs at http://victorywhiskeyjuliet.tumblr.com.

Lynn Beighley is a fiction writer stuck in a technical book writer's body. Her stories often involve deeply flawed characters and the unsatisfying meshing of the virtual and actual world. She has an MFA in Creative Writing and currently has 16 books published.

Margaret Bingel is just a writer, living in Manchester, New Hampshire. She spends her time working at her father's beer store, art modeling, and writing (when she can). She doesn't have a website or a blog yet, but who knows, maybe she'll have one in the future.

Guilie Castillo–Oriard is a Mexican writer currently exiled in the island of Curaçao. She misses Mexican food and Mexican *amabilidad*, but the laissez–faire attitude and the beaches of the

Caribbean are fair exchange. Plus, the bounty of cultural diversity inspires great culture−clash fiction. Guilie is currently revising and editing her first novel. Her short stories have appeared in *Fiction 365, Lady Ink Magazine* and *Pure Slush*. She blogs at http://guilie−castillo−oriard.blogspot.com.

John Wentworth Chapin lives and writes in Baltimore, where he is too frequently starting Project B before finishing Project A. John writes non−fiction as well as fiction. Find him on the web at http://johnwentworthchapin.com.

James Claffey hails from County Westmeath, Ireland, and lives on an avocado ranch in Carpinteria, CA with his family. He is the author of a collection of short fiction, *Blood a Cold Blue*. His website can be found at http://jamesclaffey.com.

Gay Degani has published online and in print including *The Best of Every Day Fiction* editions and her own collection, *Pomegranate Stories*. She is the founder−editor emeritus of EDF's *Flash Fiction Chronicles*, a staff editor at *Smokelong Quarterly*, and blogs at http://wordsinplace.blogspot.com where a list of her work can be found. She's had two stories nominated for Pushcart consideration and won the eleventh Annual Glass Woman Prize for her flash piece, *Something about L.A.*

Michelle Elvy is an editor and writer who has meandered from the shores of the Chesapeake to New Zealand's Bay of Islands. Michelle has published poetry, short stories and non−fiction about travel, faraway places, food, motorcycling, slow travel, the kindness of strangers and raising children in unusual places for numerous literary journals and magazines in the US, Canada, Australasia, the UK and Europe. She edits at *Flash Frontier: An Adventure in Short Fiction* and *Blue Five Notebook*. She can also be found regularly at *Awkword Paper Cut*. More about manuscript assessment and Michelle's take on editing and writing can be found at http://michelleelvy.com.

Gloria Garfunkel is the daughter of two Auschwitz survivors, which deeply affected her whole life and personality. She has a Ph.D. from Harvard University in Psychology and Social Relations, concentrating on Personality Development Studies. She was a psychotherapist for thirty years working with children, adults and families. She is currently retired, reading and writing to her heart's content. She has published many stories in journals and anthologies and hopes to eventually publish a collection of her flash fiction. You can find more of her work at her blog http://queruloussquirreldaily.blogspot.com/.

Teresa Burns Gunther has had fiction and nonfiction appear in numerous literary journals and most recently in *Northwind Magazine*, *Bookslut* and *Best New Writing 2012*. Teresa is the Editor of *The Lakeside*, an online literary magazine, and she founded Lakeshore Writers Workshop in Oakland, California where she leads creative writing workshops and classes and works one-on-one with writers. You can find links to her work at http://www.teresaburnsgunther.com/.

Gill Hoffs lives with her family and an ever-dwindling supply of Nutella in the North of England. Find Gill on Facebook or as @gillhoffs on twitter, email her a dirty joke at gillhoffs@hotmail.co.uk, or leave a clean comment at http://gillhoffs.wordpress.com/. *Wild: a collection* is out now from *Pure Slush Books*. Her non-fiction book *The Sinking of RMS Tayleur: the Lost Story of the Victorian Titanic* is out now from *Pen & Sword*. Feel free to send her chocolate.

Joanne Jagoda of Oakland, California, took an inspiring writing workshop after retiring in 2009, and launched on a long-postponed creative writing journey. Since discovering her passion for writing, she has worked non-stop on short stories, poetry and non-fiction. Her work has appeared in a number of e-zines and print anthologies, including *Pure Slush* and *Idea Gems Magazine*, and she was a poet of the month for a Jewish news weekly in Northern California. When not taking writing and poetry classes, Joanne enjoys being a writer-coach for ninth graders, Zumba, and visiting her three grandchildren in Jerusalem.

Len Kuntz is a writer from Washington State and an editor at the online literary magazine *Metazen*. His work appears widely in print and online. Find him at http://lenkuntz.blogspot.com.

Sally-Anne Macomber was born and raised in Toronto, Canada, and studied journalism at Concordia University in Montreal. Her work on high fashion and the demise of haute couture has appeared in various online and print publications in both Europe and North America. She turned to writing flash fiction in 2010, and hasn't looked back.

Jessica McHugh is an author of speculative fiction that spans the genre from horror and alternate history to epic fantasy. A member of the Horror Writers Association and a 2013 Pulp Ark nominee, she has devoted herself to novels, short stories, poetry, and playwriting. Jessica has had thirteen books published in five years, including the bestselling *Rabbits in the Garden*, *The Sky: The World* and the gritty coming-of-age thriller, *PINS*. More info on her speculations and publications can be found at http://www.jessicamchughbooks.com.

Gwendolyn Joyce Mintz is a fiction writer and aspiring photographer. Her work has appeared in various online and print publications. In other incarnations, Mintz is a writing instructor, a teddy bear maker and somebody's grandmother.

h. l. nelson is Founding Editor/Executive Director of *Cease,*

Cows lit mag and a former sidewalk mannequin. Pub credits: *PANK, Hobart, Connotation Press, Metazen, Drunk Monkeys, Red Fez, Bartleby Snopes.* She's also editing an anthology which includes stories by Aimee Bender, Roxane Gay, Lindsay Hunter and other fierce women writers. Her MFA is currently kicking her ass. Tell her what you're wearing: heather@hlnelson.com.

Mandy Nicol grew up in Melbourne, Australia and made a tree change to country Victoria in the mid–nineties – the decade, not her age. She has various animals including a flockette of pet sheep that are thankful for her vegaquarian habits. She writes short stories and loves flash fiction. *Pure Slush* is the first venue to publish her work.

Derek Osborne lives in eastern Pennsylvania. His work has appeared in *Boston Literary Magazine, Bartleby Snopes, Literary Orphans, The Linnet's Wings, Pure Slush* and many others. To read more visit http://gertrudesflat.blogspot.com, or email him at derekosborne1@gmail.com.

Vanessa Weibler Paris lives in Erie, Pa., with a guy, a girl, a boy, a bunny rabbit and a dog. She writes things both real (for work) and pretend (for fun). Her favorite things include hot peppers, bad puns, small–world stories, and tales with a twist at the end.

Gary Percesepe is Associate Editor at *New World Writing* (formerly *Mississippi Review*) and a Contributor at *The Nervous Breakdown.* Author of four books in philosophy, Percesepe's poetry, fiction, essays, and interviews have appeared in *Story Quarterly, N + 1, Salon, Mississippi Review, The Millions, Brevity, PANK, Metazen, The Brooklyner,* and other places. His collection of short stories, *Why I Did the Grocery Girl,* is forthcoming from Aqueous Books. His poetry collection *falling* and his flash fiction collection *itch* were published by *Pure Slush*

Books in late 2013. He has taught at Saint Louis University, Wittenberg University, and University of Dayton. He lives in Buffalo, New York.

Matt Potter is an Australian—born writer who keeps a part of his psyche in Berlin. Matt has been published in various places online, and he is, rather amazingly, also the founding editor of *Pure Slush*. You can find more of his work at his website: http://mattcpotter.webs.com/.

Darryl Price was born in Kentucky and educated at Thomas More College. A founding member of L. Jack Roth's Yellow Pages Poets, he has published dozens of chapbooks, and his poems have appeared in many journals. He currently edits *Olentangy Review* with his wife Melissa.

Stephen V. Ramey is an American author from New Castle, Pennsylvania. His work has appeared in many places, including *The Doctor TJ Eckleburg Review*, *The Journal of Compressed Creative Arts*, and *A Capella Zoo*. *Glass Animals*, his first collection of (very) short fiction is available from *Pure Slush Books*. Find him and more of his work at his website: http://www.stephenvramey.com.

Shane Simmons is a self—confessed coffee shop writer who believes that regardless of quality, each paragraph penned should be rewarded with sweet treats (cake, muffins, Belgian waffles, etc). London—born, he ran away to Glasgow ten years ago. Since then he has expanded his waistline and he now blogs at http://scribblingsimmons.wordpress.com/.

Kimberlee Smith is a writer whose poetry, essays, fiction, and creative nonfiction have been published in numerous literary journals and anthologies. She was awarded a residency to the Jentel Arts Program in 2013. She lives with her two daughters, two dogs, three cats, two rabbits, and nine chooks on her farm in rural Connecticut. She received her MA in English from the University of Sydney, a certificate in the Creative Writing Program through UCLA, and her BA in Journalism from the University of Southern California. She is enrolled currently in post–graduate studies at Columbia University in New York. She can do a headstand on a trampoline, kill a chook, and make hard cider from the apples in her orchard.

Andrew Stancek was born in Bratislava and saw Russian tanks occupying his homeland. His dreams of circuses and ice cream, flying and lion–taming, miracle and romance have appeared recently in print in *LA Review*, *Windsor Review* and *New Sun Rising: Stories for Japan*. Among the many online publications featuring his work are *Every Day Fiction*, *Gemini Magazine* (Flash Fiction Contest Grand Prize Winner), *fwriction*, *r.kv.r.y. quarterly literary journal*, *Tin House*, *Flash Fiction Chronicles*, *The Linnet's Wings*, *Connotation Press*, *THIS Literary Magazine*, *LA Review*, *Windsor Review*, *Thrice Fiction Magazine*, *New Sun Rising*, and *Pure Slush*.

Susan Tepper is the author of four published books of fiction and a chapbook of poetry. Her most recent title *The Merrill Diaries* (*Pure Slush Books*, July 2013) is a Novel in Stories that follow a young woman's adventures in love and lust on two continents, spanning a decade. Tepper has received nine Pushcart nominations, and one for the Pulitzer Prize in fiction. You can visit her website here: http://www.susantepper.com.

Nathaniel Tower lives in the Twin Cities with his wife and daughter. After teaching high school English for nine years, he decided to pursue a career in writing / publishing / editing. His fiction has appeared in over two hundred online and print journals. His first collection of fiction, *Nagging Wives, Foolish Husbands*, was released in 2013 through *Martian Lit*. Nathaniel is the founding and managing editor of *Bartleby Snopes Literary Magazine and Press.* Find out more about Nathaniel at http://nathanieltower.wordpress.com.

Townsend Walker lives in San Francisco. His stories have been published in over fifty literary journals and included in seven anthologies. One story won the SLO NightWriters story contest. Two were nominated for the PEN / O. Henry Award. Four were performed at the New Short Fiction Series in Hollywood. He is associate editor at *Grey Sparrow Journal.* During a career in finance he published three books, on foreign exchange, derivatives and portfolio management. Educated at Georgetown, NYU and Stanford, find his website at http://www.townsendwalker.com.

Michael Webb is continually surprised anyone is interested in what he has to say, and he blogs occasionally at http://innocentsaccidentshints.blogspot.com.

Other volumes in the *2014* series from *Pure Slush*

Visit the Pure Slush Store:
http://pureslush.webs.com/store.htm

January 2014 Vol. 1
ISBN: 978−1−925101−03−4

February 2014 Vol. 2
ISBN: 978−1−925101−14−0

April 2014 Vol. 4
ISBN: 978−1−925101−27−0

May 2014 Vol. 5
ISBN: 978−1−925101−30−0

June 2014 Vol. 6
ISBN: 978−1−925101−34−8

July 2014 Vol. 7
ISBN: 978−1−925101−37−9

www.ingramcontent.com/pod-product-compliance
Lightning Source LLC
Chambersburg PA
CBHW052143170626
46812CB00004B/1570